THE NEW BIZARRO AUTHOR SERIES

PRESENTS

Janitor
of
Planet Anilingus

ANDREW WAYNE ADAMS

Eraserhead Press
Portland, OR

THE NEW BIZARRO AUTHOR SERIES
An Imprint of Eraserhead Press

ERASERHEAD PRESS
205 NE BRYANT
PORTLAND, OR 97211

WWW.ERASERHEADPRESS.COM

ISBN: 1-62105-069-6

Printed in the USA.

Editor's Note

A book about a planet where everyone licks butts? And they *want* to? Yes. It's got some stuff to say about religion in the middle of that? Yes. When I asked Andy if he had anything to send for consideration for this year's New Bizarro Author Series, he sent me that. Now I present it to you. It's only obliquely related to the act of anilingus. Mostly. (Okay, there's anilingus—how could there *not* be?)

Actually, this story was great from its first draft. Andy's style is easy to read, funny, intelligent, and skillful. He's crafted a story about self-discovery (through, uh… anilingus) and its inevitability—even in the face of happy ignorance—that entertains, lampoons, questions accepted beliefs, and pulls at the human bits of your heart. And it's all so weird. This is an author with tremendous potential.

Janitor of Planet Anilingus will make you laugh, cringe, and think at the same time. I found myself imagining everything I read as if I were watching one of the most ridiculously awesome movies I'd ever seen. I hope you enjoy the same sensation (it was crazy!).

I'm happy to present Andrew Wayne Adams' book as part of the New Bizarro Author Series. The NBAS strives to bring new voices in bizarro fiction to our readers. It serves as an opportunity to introduce you to new writers, and introduce them into the world of being an author. Eraserhead Press is happy to bring new, weird voices to you in the hopes that these authors will prove themselves to be strong members of the bizarro community and continue to entertain you for years to come. The publishing of this book marks the beginning of a one year proving period. Please help support our NBAS writers in their endeavors by telling your friends about their cool new books. The book you hold is only one of several hundred that must be sold in order for this author to continue on his path. We hope you help him along as best as you can. Thank you.

~~Kevin Shamel

For Blake Davis

MONDAY

FIRST SHIFT

A mutant bee stung Jack in his sleep, and he awoke with an erection.

The bee reclined on Jack's bicep and watched him shake off sleep. Two voluptuous breasts overflowed from its thorax; its stinger was a tumescent penis.

"Good morning, cupid," Jack said to the mutant insect.

The cupid blew him a kiss and flew away.

He reached down and felt his erection. It was at maximum rigidity. He sighed. The cupids had particularly potent stings this time of year. It was the late part of Lent and the planet was deserted, stripped of its usual pool of revelers. For forty days Jack was the planet's sole inhabitant, and by the time a cupid found him, its payload of aphrodisiac, in want of release, had stewed to an incandescent intensity.

The erection would last hours. Nothing could make it go away.

It was a nuisance, and the one downside to working during Lent. In all other respects, these six weeks were his favorite. He enjoyed being the only person on the planet, and he got paid overtime.

One more week and Lent was over, and then the cupids would not bother him. His only trouble then would be the hundreds of thousands of people licking each other's assholes day and night. They blanketed the planet, an orgy visible from space. Nonstop until next Lent.

Jack rolled out of his cot. He stood a moment and let his hand scratch at random body parts. He walked from the bedroom to the bathroom, from the bathroom to the kitchen, and from the kitchen back to the bedroom—urinating in the toilet, taking an egg from the refrigerator, and sitting on his cot (the only furniture) to eat the egg (cracked raw into his mouth). The toilet, the refrigerator, and the cot were all within five feet of each other, the three rooms really one room. With breakfast finished, he retreated to his library for a few moments of quiet reflection before beginning his day (to get to the library, he shifted slightly on his cot so that he faced the two or three magazines stacked on the radiator). His eyes rested on the cover of *Popular Pope*.

Suddenly it was time to go to work.

His normal uniform consisted of nothing but a pair of lace underwear and a bowtie. It was crucial that no irregularity should sully the planet's atmosphere of total debauchery, and a stinky janitor intruding upon the middle of an orgy would certainly do so. The job even required him to practice erotic body language as he went about his work, movements choreographed to make dusting and mopping look sexy. And if some random reveler stole a lick of his ass, he had to pretend to like it, then extricate himself as expediently as possible.

While the planet was deserted, he did not have to wear lace underwear and a bowtie. He did not have to arch his spine suggestively as he stood to empty a dustpan. No one sent a surprise tongue groping for his asshole. He wore plain blue coveralls and whistled while he worked.

A cupid found him. It rubbed its mutant breasts against his left bicep. The bicep was the size of a grapefruit. Jack had the physique of a bodybuilder—another job requirement.

He let the cupid sting him. He pretended his erection was an imaginary friend named Excalibur.

"It's a beautiful day, Excalibur," he said.

At 8:00 a.m. sharp, Jack clocked in to work. To do this, he looked at the sun, where Vatican Headquarters was visible as a tiny black wart in the center of the burning orange. A beam from the Vatican scanned his retinas and took a brainwave reading, and the system clocked him in.

The Boss's head popped out of the ground.

"Good morning, Jack," he said.

Bishop Eichmann wore the violet skullcap of his office, this atop a horseshoe of hair dyed violently to mask its early gray. His face was smooth and fat. An immaculately groomed Hitler mustache loomed like a chimney over the noxious bonfire of his lips.

Jack lay on his belly so that he was level with the Boss's head. It was a required gesture of deference.

"Jack, I hardly need remind you, but I am going to anyway: This is the final week before we reopen, and it is your duty to God to see that Planet Anilingus is ready. Last quarter's review shows Anilingus as our most popular resort—it's even surpassed Sodomy, somehow, although I don't think that will last; these fads can never compete for long with the old institutions. For the time being, however, more are flocking to Anilingus than to any other planet."

A blade of grass tickled Jack's nose.

"These men and women haven't licked an asshole in six weeks," the Bishop continued. "All they are dreaming of now is a return to Anilingus. They're drooling for paradise, and we must deliver. I'm talking true Eden, Jack—as in, not one goddamn dust bunny on the planet, and every cobblestone, every leaf, shined to look like a scale from the reptilian skin of God. Can you handle that?"

Jack said, "I'm on top of things."

"If you fuck up, I'll have you peeling potatoes on Vore."

The Boss's head turned into dirt and grass. It had

been dirt and grass all along, actually, only temporarily becoming Bishop Eichmann's head through the miracle of transubstantiation. Jack stood, watching the grass spring back. The Boss could have taken shape in the clouds or the trees, but because he liked Jack to be prostrate on the ground, he never entered into anything above knee-level.

"I wouldn't mind peeling potatoes on Vore," Jack said to no one.

Jack aimed the spray bottle at the leaf. He squeezed the trigger. A frothy jet of cleaner hit the leaf. The cleaner ran to the edge, dripped. It was blue and smelled of ammonia and steel. Jack wiped the leaf with a towel. The leaf was clean.

The towel was of a style called "1950s American Kitchen"—threadbare but sound, somehow always subliminally damp, its muted design a tessellation of oven mitts, candlesticks, and Christmas turkeys. The towel was one of several hundred of its kind that Jack had found among his issued supplies when he was first assigned here. Other mysteries he found: a rake with blood on it; an aerosol can that sprayed leeches; a tall ladder whose top vanished gradually into fog; twelve bowling balls; a stack of diaries written in Latin. He inherited all of this from his predecessor. It looked like nothing new had been added in decades.

Jack moved to the next leaf. He sprayed it, wiped it. It was clean.

He vacuumed the trunk of the tree, vacuumed the grass beneath the tree, and moved to the next tree. It was the last in the copse. Adjoining the copse, to be cleaned next, was a courtyard of marble made baroque with stairs, terraces, planters, birdbaths, wading pools... all this surrounding a mammoth fountain carved of gold. In the fountain, parabolas of water spouted from between the arched buttocks of lordotic figures in a ring, the water falling inward to meet a lotus of tongues at the center. The water, like all water, was

12

holy.

The place—copse, courtyard, fountain, a few subterranean wine cellars and saunas—was known as Coccyx Grove. A week from now it would be one of the planet's most virulent hotbeds of decadence.

Jack stood at the fountain and watched the ropes of water surging from gold sphincter to gold tongue. During Lent, the fountain was always turned off.

Someone had turned it on.

Jack was not the only person on Planet Anilingus.

He approached the fountain. Unconsciously, he held his bottle of cleaner before him like a gun, ready to spray chemical pain into the face of he knew not what. He strained his ears to hear over the fountain's rushing water.

Something splashed, something giggled.

He reached the edge of the fountain and stopped. His heart was pounding. Inside his coveralls, his erect penis shuddered with each pulse of blood. It pushed straight out on the crotch of his pants, protruding beyond the lip of the fountain, over the crystalline water.

A hand emerged from the water and encircled Jack's erection.

Reflexively, he sprayed blue cleaner, the bottle aimed nowhere.

Attached to the hand was a woman. She gazed up at Jack with an expressionless face. She was nude and completely hairless.

"I have something for you," she said.

Jack said, "I am thinking of spraying blue chemicals in your eyes."

"Don't do that," she said. "I have something to give you."

"What?"

She squeezed the fist with Jack's erection in it. "Him."

"You can't give him to me. He's already mine. His name

is Excalibur."

"No. You've never truly owned him until now." She let go. "Now he is yours."

Jack sprayed blue chemicals in her eyes.

She cursed, but not in pain. "I told you not to do that."

"Why aren't your eyeballs melting?" Jack did well at concealing alarm, but a trace of it still entered his voice. "Who are you? What are doing here?"

She blinked, the corner of each eye raining fat blue tears that smelled of ammonia and steel. "My name is Nimue." A smile flickered upon the blankness of her face. "I'm sorry. This must be very shocking. I will explain everything. Only allow me first to dry from my bath."

Rising from the water, she stepped past Jack over the lip of the fountain. She walked a short distance and paused within a circle of strong sunlight. Jack studied the beads of water that hung on her hairless skin. The water dried in the sunlight—dried within an instant, droplets shrinking at time-lapse speed, seeming to tumble inward into her pores.

She asked his name. He told her.

She said, "Our lives are in danger, Jack."

SECOND SHIFT

Nimue turned, seeming startled by some sound Jack couldn't hear. Her eyes roamed the light and shadow of Coccyx Grove, nostrils flaring as if vigilant for a scent she knew and hated. Jack started to speak, and she held up a finger to quiet him. She pivoted slowly, scanning.

Jack noticed for the first time the gaping hole in the small of her back.

The hole, about the size of a fist, was dead center at the base of her spine. Its edges were puckered and smooth, like scar tissue or a loose sphincter. The light penetrated not far into the aperture; some slight moisture glistened deep within.

Nimue said, quietly, "I think we should go."

"Why? What's going on?" Jack, without knowing it, was flexing every major muscle group. His pupils were dilated, and his skin prickled.

"There is a depraved maniac stalking me." Her lips cut to a smile for a single frame, then resumed their flatness. "He has tried to kill me eight times already. I think I must be genetically similar to a cat. Nine lives."

Jack did not know what a cat was. Some mythological beast. It sounded fierce.

"I might not survive the next attempt. And when he finishes with me, he'll come after you. Do you have nine lives?"

Jack barely had one life. He said so. He said, "I probably have some fractional amount of a life." He heard leaves rustle and wondered if it was the depraved maniac. "Is there some mythological beast that has a fractional amount of a life?"

"A mouse," Nimue said. She studied him. "You are very muscular."

"I'm the janitor," he said. "I have to look good in lace underwear and a bowtie."

"Have you ever fought for your life?"

There was the time he had almost committed suicide, but he didn't think that counted. "No," he said. "I've never faced an external enemy."

"Prepare to."

Nimue refused to stay in Coccyx Grove any longer. The maniac was near, she said. Jack saw a shadow move and said, "My truck's right outside."

He expected her to go retrieve whatever clothing she had stripped before bathing in the fountain, but she moved immediately to leave with him. Jack realized that she had no clothes. Perpetual nudity was the norm for revelers on Anilingus, but Jack, in his shock, had not thought to connect this hairless naked woman with that bunch. She still had not explained herself.

Speeding away from Coccyx Grove on a highway paved with gold, Jack glanced at the expressionless woman in the passenger seat and said, "Tell me who you are."

She didn't speak for a long minute. Jack couldn't tell if she'd heard him. Finally she said, "I'm a Roman Catholic, married, with two children—a boy and a girl. I enjoy anilingus, cunnilingus, fellatio, sodomy, and feet."

Jack said, "Sounds statistically average and in compliance."

"My husband wanted to vacation on Sadomasochism this year, but I was still recovering from our trip there last year, so I came alone to Anilingus." She fell silent again. Something about her bald head made her look massively intelligent. "Just before Lent, when everyone was licking ass at a frantic rate, I coupled with a random man as he emerged from the desert. He claimed to be a crucifix salesman. As he was servicing me, he stabbed me in the spine with a sharpened crucifix." She turned to display the gaping hole that Jack had noticed earlier. "My spinal fluid leaked out onto the ground. I believe several dozen blades of grass absorbed the fluid and became sentient. They likely have a fledgling civilization by now."

Jack said, "I will have to be careful next time I mow."

"The crucifix salesman rolled my body into a pond and left me for dead. But the pond water, like all water, was holy—perhaps blessed by the Pope himself, for the miracle it performed on me was truly awesome. The water cauterized my wound; it gave me back the spinal fluid I had lost, replacing it with itself—my neurons run on holy water, now—and it became as air for me to breathe until I regained consciousness and swam to the surface. I met a unicorn upon the shore and rode him to safety."

Jack did not know what a unicorn was.

"I don't know how long I was at the bottom of that pond, but by the time I rode the unicorn back to Cecum City, everyone had left the planet. Everyone but the crucifix salesman. He lives on this planet, in secret. In a cave full of bones."

"What cave? I am intimately familiar with this planet, and I've never encountered a cave full of bones." Jack alternated his eyes between the road and the woman. "How did all of this go on without the Vatican knowing?" Jack needed to urinate. "What's a unicorn?"

Nimue ignored his questions. "Somehow, the maniac learned I was still alive, and he's been trying to finish me off ever since."

She peered out the window. They were passing through a vastness of tidy grass, a landscape unnaturally green and smooth—like the surface of a billiard table—and studded at odd intervals with statues, all famed sculptures that dealt with man's relation to man's anus. Coming up on the right was Monty Cantsin's *The Stinker*—which was simply Rodin's *The Thinker* with another figure poised to release

17

a fart into the eponymous contemplator's face—and on the left, artist unknown, was *The Gates of Heaven*—a work in bronze depicting the puffy ring of a sphincter muscle twisted into a tight trefoil knot, rogue tongues crawling like slugs along its convolutions.

Nimue observed the sculptures, her face a mixture of admiration and amusement, of contempt and boredom; it was hard to read her mind in the infinitesimal fluctuations of her expression. Her nakedness, her hairlessness, seemed to strip her of personality. She looked at Jack, gaze the same as if he were one of the passing statues, and said, "Where are we going?"

"Janitor's station. We can defend ourselves there. And, I have eggs in the fridge. I could really use an egg right now. Maybe two eggs."

He pushed the truck to top speed. Statues streamed past on both sides of the golden highway. Ahead, one of the statues moved. It wasn't a statue.

"It's the depraved maniac," Nimue said.

The depraved maniac lifted a handheld rocket launcher and fired at Jack's truck.

Jack had never before been fired at by a rocket launcher. The experience was astounding: the neat, rational load of fire unleashed along its inexorable trajectory; the hiss, the roar, as the instant before death contracted, expanded, got stuck in a loop, freeze-framed; the rocket unzipping the air, tweezing apart its interlocked molecules... groping ahead, not blindly, but with utter acuity, for Jack, to unzip his carbon chains...

He twisted the wheel. The truck bounced off the side of the road, veering straight for the darkness between two giant granite butt cheeks. He twisted the wheel some more.

The rocket hit the truck, and the truck rode upward on a mushroom of flame.

Nimue threw herself at Jack, wrapped him in her arms,

kicked open the door, and said, "Hold on." Jack held on, and Nimue leaped from the airborne truck.

They were a hundred feet or more above the ground. Below them, flame boiled up like orange-black cauliflower growing in fast-forward.

There was a mechanical whine, and a thick metal rod sprouted from the hole in Nimue's back. Helicopter blades, black and military-looking, unfolded from the rod and started to spin. Jack and Nimue lifted into the air, evading the column of fire.

The depraved maniac tracked their getaway. Jack saw him fire another rocket. The rocket hissed like a stadium of laughing snakes.

"Aghhhhh!" Jack screamed. "Dive!

His guts pirouetted as Nimue maneuvered into a sudden freefall. The rocket exploded overhead, became a rain of laughing shrapnel. Nimue banked hard to the right. Shrapnel fell into the whirl of her helicopter blades and ricocheted in all directions.

Jack had his arms locked around Nimue's torso, her breasts on his head. Mucus seeped from the hole in her back, coating the base of the helicopter rotor. The spinning of the blades sent vibrations shuddering through Jack's ribcage. He was aware that he had an erection, and he wondered if a cupid had stung him amidst the confusion of all these near-death experiences. Or, maybe he was just actually turned on.

The maniac fired one more rocket—but they were already out of range, and the maniac knew it; the rocket was for show, an expression of frustration.

Nimue spun her blades at double speed, accelerating away.

Jack felt wetness at his crotch. He had ejaculated in his coveralls.

THIRD SHIFT

Jack looked at the sun.

The cum was drying in his pants, adhering flesh to fabric. His boner had not gone away. Far behind them, black smoke curled off the horizon, and Jack thought he could smell his burning truck. Nimue's nipples raked across his scalp. He had tried several times to speak to her, but it was impossible over the thrum of the helicopter blades. She sped through the air, following the golden highway. Jack kept looking back to see if there were any signs of pursuit.

Against the evening sun, Vatican Headquarters posed like a mole on a fashion model. Jack fixed it in his gaze. He sent out a distress signal with his mind. He had a fuzzy imagining of some bored deacon perking up at his terminal as the panicked brainwaves blipped across it: MAYDAY MAYDAY MAYDAY. TROUBLE ON ANILINGUS. MAYDAY MAYDAY MAYDAY. I NEED TO URINATE. (It was hard to control what got picked up in a brainwave scan.) The deacon would ring a big brass bell, and ten to twenty other deacons, weary but alert, would jump up from their bunks, slide down a pole through a hole in the floor, and barely clear the opening bay door as their emergency vehicle wailed into the night (in Jack's imagining, there was such a thing as "night" on the sun).

He waited for some sign of rescue. He didn't know what he was waiting for. Sirens? Flashing lights? His mommy?

There was none of that.

The expanse of statue-studded landscape ended, its plane of pastel green giving way to a neon confusion of polychromatic fungi. The revelers called it Boogie Wonderland, and it was an acquired taste: a dense forest of gargantuan mushrooms... rivers of hallucinogenic slime... the warm murk choked with a gastrointestinal fragrance, and mechanical bats flapping along preprogrammed routes.

Jack still needed to clean Boogie Wonderland. He made a mental note: bring gloves, galoshes. He planned his custodial assault: top to bottom, back to front. Agitate all dust and grime into the open, then apprehend it with suction, moisture, static charge. His arsenal was diverse, versatile. He was a conqueror of entropy.

Nimue leaked some secretion from her nipples, and it ran into Jack's eyes and burned them, reminding him of the situation on his hands. He no longer felt so powerful against entropy. He felt rather like a plaything of bedlam.

"Where are you taking us?" Jack shouted above the chop of the helicopter blades.

"We are still en route to the janitor's station."

He saw that they were. Nimue had turned off the main highway and was following an unpaved trail that led away from Boogie Wonderland. Jack wondered how she knew where the station was.

"I scanned your brainwaves," she answered.

Jack wondered how she knew what he had just been thinking.

"I scanned your brainwaves," she answered.

The janitor's station was a large complex nestled within a ring of low hills. The hills kept the station hidden from guests of the planet, because to see the station might shatter their illusion of hedonistic paradise. The complex had once been a prison, and it still looked like one: walls of black stone, every tiny window and cyclopean door crosshatched with bars of unassailable iron. The prison was the vestige of an older epoch, before Anilingus was Anilingus. Back then, the planet was called Panopticon 4. The galaxy had been a very different place. No one was certain what those times were like. Most of the details had been expunged from the history books, and then the history books had been expunged from existence, and now there was only the occasional sensationalistic reference to the Old Eon made in magazines. Audience studies showed that unexpected mention of the Old Eon caused a spike of adrenaline in readers, and this was good for selling copies of *Popular Pope* and *Body and Blood*.

Nimue decelerated to a hover and dropped slowly into contact with the ground. She released Jack from her hold. His body felt gelatinous from its vibrating trip through the air. He wanted to throw himself on the ground and celebrate it with kisses, inhale its perfume.

Mechanical whirs and clicks rang out like a song from Nimue's body as her helicopter rotor folded up and retracted, sucked back into the orifice near her sacrum. She looked around. "These hills are good concealment. The maniac will never know this place even exists."

"Unless he can scan brainwaves," Jack said. He glared at Nimue. "Apparently it's a talent more common than I realized."

"Not common at all," she said. "I am unique." She didn't look at him as she spoke, gazing instead at the janitor's station. Assessing this new citadel was more important than their conversation, it seemed. "I am the next step in evolution."

"Can you hear every thought I have?"

"No."

He narrowed his eyes at her. He thought, I HATE YOU I HATE YOU I HATE YOU—not because he actually hated her (he was still getting to know her), but because it was a strong enough message that its impact would be immediate and recognizable. He expected her to flinch. Or to smirk, at least. But her expressionless expression didn't waver.

"You didn't just hear me thinking something?"

"No." As if annoyed, she finally gave him her full attention. "I was only able to scan your brainwaves because I absorbed a small amount of your semen when you ejaculated in your pants. A little bit soaked through the fabric and into my skin. Your erection acts as the transmitter, and I use your gametes to tune to the proper frequency. I'm no longer getting a signal because the little bit of semen I absorbed from you is already depleted. Your antenna is still up; if you were to give me more semen, you could speak to me without ever opening your mouth."

Jack looked at Excalibur—his "antenna"—and blushed. He was not a self-conscious person, but something about Nimue disturbed his comfort. He said, "A cupid must have stung me. It's normal. I can't help it."

"Of course."

"During Lent, I'm the only one they have to target, and by the time they find me, they have a serious case of blue balls. But unlike their usual customers, I don't particularly enjoy being injected with a tidal wave of aphrodisiac, particularly when it's several times more potent than it should be."

Nimue seemed to lose interest. She turned back to her inspection of the grounds. "Do you have food?" she said. "Where are your living quarters?"

"Follow me," Jack said, and started toward the enormous keep.

He approached the main entrance but stopped before entering. A dented aluminum trailer sat on concrete blocks near the imposing door of the old prison. Pink flamingos and sunflower pinwheels stood from the grass on crooked stakes.

"Home," Jack said.

She gazed up at the black fortress that loomed over the trailer.

"Supply closet," Jack explained. "I have to clean an entire planet. It takes a lot of towels."

Jack gave a tour of his home. "Bedroom, bathroom, kitchen," he said, pointing first to his cot, then to his toilet, and finally to his refrigerator.

Nimue went straight to the refrigerator. The fridge held nothing but eggs—hundreds of them, kept not in cartons but in one communal heap, the summit of which nearly reached the feebly burning bulb screwed into the fridge's ceiling. Nimue took an egg from the heap, held it a foot above her mouth, and cracked it open. The yolk was a soft blur of yellow that flashed between eggshell and lips. She repeated the motion with two more, three more eggs. Thick drippings of albumen ran from chin to neck, from neck to breasts, a transparent glaze upon her nipples. She cracked egg after egg into her mouth, mechanically and with no sign of stopping. Emptied shells fell everywhere as she tossed them over her shoulder.

Jack never had company—ever, in his life?—and so didn't know if Nimue's behavior was typical of a guest. He watched patiently. He sat in the library and read an article in *Body and Blood* denouncing the sandwich as a heretical invention. He did not agree with the article. Nimue slurped and gurgled. Jack peeked around her into the refrigerator and saw that half his eggs were gone. He too wanted an egg but was afraid of what might happen if he butted in.

Without warning, she finished her binge and closed the refrigerator. She turned to Jack and said, "Water." Then added, "Preferably in liquid form."

"There's a well out back."

She stepped outside. Jack, before following, cracked

open the fridge and darted a hand inside. He smuggled two eggs into his mouth, shell and all. It felt like theft.

Behind the trailer were a well, a chicken coop, and a lawn chair. Nimue was nowhere in sight. Jack heard splashing. He went to the edge of the well, leaning over the low stone wall to look inside. The water shimmered far below. A plume of bubbles broke its surface. Something was rising from the depths.

Nimue exploded from the water like a porpoise. Her hands and feet grasped the wall, and she climbed the slick stone with such speed that Jack had to throw himself out of the way before she bulldozed into him. He hit the ground and found himself facing the same patch of dirt and grass that had earlier been Bishop Eichmann's head.

Nimue shot from the well, landed skillfully on her feet.

"I am fed and watered," she said. She sat in the lawn chair by the chicken coop. She looked at Jack, who was still on the ground by the well. "Come, gather near." Her hairless body shone with water, cold and clean. "I wish to pass the time in conversation."

Jack looked at the sun. Nimue seemed confident that they were safe here, but Jack was still nervous. He expected sudden death to swoop in at any second. He hated dealing with Vatican staff, but he also hated getting fired at with rockets. He needed reinforcements.

But there was no response from the Vatican. It was mystifying. Usually nothing escaped their attention. Jack sent the distress signal again and again, staring daggers at the sun.

If they heard, they didn't care.

Jack said to Nimue, "We could probably find weapons in the supply closet."

She said, "The air feels so wonderful on my skin."

She would not talk about the psychopath stalking them.

25

She sat in the lawn chair with her legs crossed and talked about the sunset, the hills, the silence. Jack sat on the ground beside her, his back against the chicken coop. He said, "I feel extremely vulnerable to death right now."

She said, "I see a cupid. How cute!"

He said, "Don't you think we should discuss how to best fight for our lives?"

She said, "Can I meet your chicken?"

Cleopatra was a quiet bird, but she had clucked a few times while they sat there, and each cluck drew a look of blank-faced bemusement from Nimue. The chicken had clucked again just now, pushing Nimue's curiosity to critical mass.

"If I show you my chicken, will you agree to get serious?"

"Let's see it," she said. She uncrossed her legs and crossed them the other way.

The coop was large, perhaps the size of a doghouse built for a bullmastiff with gigantism. Jack opened it, letting in the orange evening sun. Dust circulated languidly in the light. Against one wall was a small television playing *The Price Is Right* on mute. Cleopatra sat opposite the TV in a cushy armchair. She gave Jack and Nimue a perfunctory glance, then turned back to the game show (a single taped episode looping endlessly).

"What beautiful feathers," Nimue said.

A chute ran from the back of the chair to the floor. Cleopatra clucked, and an instant later there rolled a fresh egg down the chute. It came to rest among several dozen others already upon the floor.

Nimue reached into the coop and took an egg. "Shame there wasn't a cock around to fertilize these." She rubbed the egg down the midline of her torso.

A contestant on *The Price Is Right* was excited and kissed the host.

Jack watched Nimue slide the egg down to her naked genitals. A large-breasted cupid landed on his bicep and stabbed him with its penis-stinger.

"Such beautiful feathers," Nimue said again, staring at

Cleopatra.

Cleopatra turned from the TV and regarded Nimue.

Excalibur groaned against the restraint of Jack's clothing.

Nimue pushed the egg between her labia. The egg went up inside.

The contestant on *The Price Is Right* bared her breasts to the host.

Cleopatra clucked.

Jack had never before been in an orgy with a mysterious woman and a chicken. The experience was astounding: Nimue climbing into the chicken coop, into the golden and dust-filled light, seeming effervescent in an aura of motes; Cleopatra rising from her armchair, the sensual bulge of her breast feathers an analogue to the human breasts now bouncing in sex on the muted television; woman and bird reaching for Jack to draw him into the coop, the assertive fingers of Nimue already at work on the zipper of his coveralls... his last glance at the sun showing it half eaten by the horizon... the Vatican eclipsed by Anilingus as night replaced dusk...

Jack's first instinct was to bury Excalibur in Nimue's vagina, but she forbade it, insisting that they adhere to the spirit of the planet. She arched her buttocks toward him. As he licked her anus, he kept a wary eye on the hole at the base of her spine, just inches away. His mind flinched from the vivid fancy of helicopter blades erupting into his skull.

While Jack serviced her, Nimue serviced Cleopatra. The chicken clucked a song and belched eggs from its rear. Broken eggs coated the floor, smashed beneath the wriggling threesome. Feathers hung in the air.

Jack found himself on the receiving end. He had never taken pleasure from the random tongues that sometimes sneaked between his butt cheeks as he went about his work among the planet's rabble. Those unwanted licks were an inconvenience—like the attention of mosquitoes. But what Nimue now gave him was different. Her tongue snaked into his rectum as if it had a right to be there, forging ahead in a fever of Manifest Destiny. It filled him up. He could see it pushing out against the wall of his belly. It had to be three feet long.

He closed his eyes against the pleasure. He did not know if it even *was* pleasure—but that ambiguity was, in itself, pleasurable.

White light exploded behind his lids.

TUESDAY

FIRST SHIFT

Jack awoke on his cot. He lay there for a moment while the world streamed in. Pieces of last night shifted through his memory. He sat up. There was no sign of Nimue. Everything was quiet. He had to be at work in five minutes.

His guts made a noise. He had never before heard such a noise. A concerned hand went to his belly, senses tuned to inside for some further signal. The signal came, and he rushed from cot to toilet.

Within his rectum, all law and order collapsed.

He thought back to Nimue's yardstick of tongue. His diarrhea proceeded like a state of emergency, and he wondered: Did she give me a disease? Is this herpes? He knew the names of the ancient venereal demons, but not their characteristics. There were those few at the top of the infernal hierarchy, damned names that evaded him now. He feared them.

"Nimue?" he called. "*Nimue?*" He wanted to ask her: Did you give me syphilis?

Work started in one minute. The turmoil in his colon showed no sign of ending. He pinched it off and rose from the toilet. The riot migrated from lower intestines to upper, creating mass confusion. He felt on the verge of vomiting, then an instant later found himself ravenously hungry. There seemed to be a colony of balloons inflating and deflating inside of him.

The hunger drove him to the fridge.

Empty. Not a single egg left.

This morning was too cruel.

Suddenly it was time to go to work.

Jack looked at the sun, wondering if it even recognized his existence anymore. He was actually relieved (first time ever) to see Bishop Eichmann's head building itself from the dirt and grass. Trying not to shit his pants, he dropped to the ground to be level with the Boss's head.

No sooner had the Boss finished transubstantiating than he said, "You're fired, Jack."

Jack had not even had time to open his mouth. He pretended not to hear what the Boss had just said; it was too much for his mind to process right now. "I'm in a lot of trouble."

"Yes, you are. You're fired."

"Look, I can't work today. I'm really sick."

"You can't work today because you're fired."

"Why?"

"You completely fell off the map yesterday. Snuck away from work in the middle of the day. Where the hell were you?"

"I can explain everything—"

"What I want to know is, how long were you getting away with this dereliction of duty before we finally caught you? And how did you do it? Rest assured, your methods will be found out by the Inquisitional Board..."

"I have no idea what you're talking about." Jack's usual patience was in short supply, and the Bishop was getting on his nerves. "Listen, I'm trying to tell you: Anilingus is in jeopardy."

The Boss was quiet. Jack supposed it was his way of saying: "Go on."

Jack said, "I'm not the only one on the planet. I encountered a strange woman yesterday while cleaning Coccyx Grove. And she told me there was a psychopath loose on Anilingus. And then I encountered the psychopath. He blew up my truck with a rocket."

"That truck was company property."

"I tried contacting Headquarters repeatedly. No one answered."

"We have no record of any of this. If you had tried to signal us, we would have known. You are clearly lying. I don't know where you really disappeared to yesterday, or what really became of the company truck—but I do know that there is no one but you on this planet. Our sensors would detect any other presence. Your tall tale is an insult to the sophistication of God's technological apparatus."

"But the woman is here, somewhere. Wait." He called for her.

"There is no woman."

"I think she gave me a disease…"

The Boss assumed a curt tone, signaling that he was through with Jack's foolishness. "Your replacement shall be arriving shortly; ready a vessel. You are to train him in his duties and assist him for the remainder of Lent. Then you will be collected by the Inquisitional Board. We will be keeping a close watch on you; do not try to escape."

The Boss's head turned back into dirt and grass.

Thinking an egg might ease his nausea, Jack went around back to the chicken coop. Cleopatra was sure to have a few fresh ones for him.

The chicken glanced quickly at him as he opened the coop, then went back to watching TV. Jack stood a moment and watched the taped episode of *The Price Is Right*. He waited for the part where the excited contestant kissed the host, bared her breasts, and initiated intercourse on live television. He waited, but the segment was missing. In fact, he did not recall ever having seen that part of the episode until last night.

Cleopatra clucked, and an egg rolled down the chute. The chicken paid no notice as Jack took the egg; she acted completely normal, as if nothing had happened last night. Perhaps nothing had. Perhaps he had dreamt the whole adventure. Had he really met a naked woman in Coccyx Grove and escaped with her from a rocket-wielding stranger? Had three feet of tongue really slithered into his bowels?

He heard splashing. He turned.

Nimue came leaping out of the well. She must have been down there the whole time. He watched her skin dry, the bright water swirling into her hairless pores. She approached him, took the egg he had been holding, and ate it. She reached down and felt his erection, which he had not been aware he had.

She said, "Good morning, Excalibur. It's a beautiful day."

Jack said, "Did you give me syphilis?"

Nimue walked past him and leaned into the chicken coop. She stroked Cleopatra's wing and said, "Good morning." Cleopatra gave her an egg. Nimue came out of the coop and seated herself in the lawn chair. She rubbed the egg along the base of her neck as if it were an ice cube on a hot day. She looked at Jack and said, "Shouldn't you be at work?"

"I got fired."

His guts made a noise; it sounded like a novice tuba player was practicing scales in his duodenum. Nimue creased her brow. "You need to eat," she said. "Here." She held out the egg that she had been cooling herself with.

Jack took it, ate it quickly. "The Vatican says you don't exist."

"They're silly. Why did they fire you?"

"Because of you."

"But I don't exist."

"Exactly. They think I was just skipping out on work yesterday. They don't believe my story. They know nothing of you or the killer. I think I might be crazy. They are going to torture me, probably."

"I will protect you."

"You don't exist."

"Have another egg." She held one toward him. He had not seen her take it from the coop; she had not left her seat. The egg was just suddenly in her hand, as if she'd brought it out of some hiding place. It was warm and slick.

He ate it, shell and all.

SECOND SHIFT

Jack's replacement arrived at noon.

He did not have the physique of a janitor. He was pasty, he was pudgy, and he was going to look nightmarish in lace underwear and a bowtie. He would ruin any orgy he crossed paths with. And he didn't seem to realize it.

"Hi there!" he said, grinning and offering his hand. "I'm Tommy!"

Jack shook the hand. It was deformed and slimy with blood.

"Oh, sorry!" Tommy said, seeing the blood he had gotten on Jack. "This was my first full-body transubstantiation. Guess I'm still getting the hang of it!"

Jack had slaughtered a pig for the new guy to transubstantiate into. Pig flesh was the easiest to work into human substance, and Jack had in his supply closet a small herd of swine for use as vessels during full-body visits. A full-body visit was rare. Jack had never before had to slaughter a pig. It was an astounding experience.

Tommy stared at his hand as if trying to focus some psychic power on it. The hand was still half pig, gnarled bits of hoof and fingernail stuck like shrapnel in a pot roast of palmistry lines. Tommy moved the flesh with his mind, and the hand became a little less grotesque—instead of half pig, a quarter pig.

"Oh well," he said. "I'll keep working on it."

"Make it quick," Jack said. "Since you'll be staying here, this is now your full-time body. Your hand might get stuck that way. I don't really know. I've never transubstantiated."

"Really? Not even partial-body?"

"I'm just a janitor."

Tommy smiled. "A janitor! That's what I'm gonna be!"

"I know. I'll be training you. You're taking my job."

"Ah, I see," he nodded. "Sounds good!"

"The job that was mine for seven years."

"Wow! Seven years!"

"I will probably be getting tortured by this time next week."

"Oh, wow. Well, good luck!"

Tommy had an erection. A cupid had stung him. Jack wondered if his penis was half pig. It would seem to fit him.

Nimue came out of the trailer. Tommy's eyes lit up, and he froze for a moment, stunned by the naked woman. Then he broke away toward her in an inattentive beeline that sent him crashing as his legs tangled with a pink flamingo and a sunflower pinwheel. He struggled back to his feet, undeterred, and as he came into range lifted his mutant hand for Nimue to shake.

"Hi there!" he said, a little out of breath. "I'm Tommy! Tommy Eichmann!"

Eichmann.

Somehow, Jack hadn't noticed. Tommy looked just like the Boss.

Nimue shook his hand.

It was the lack of a Hitler mustache that made the resemblance hard to detect. That little broom of hair was an indelible piece of the Bishop's features.

What relation had Tommy to the Bishop? Son? Nephew? Developmentally challenged younger brother? Jack even toyed with the idea that Tommy was the Bishop himself, mustache shaved as disguise and years shed from his face by the simple trade of sourness for cheer. The possibility filled him with a swimming sense of unreality. He imagined Tommy as the Bishop in disguise… the Bishop as the Pope in disguise… the Pope as God in disguise… and God as inscrutable and malefic, bent only upon the sabotage of Jack's mind. The thought made his flesh crawl. He turned away from it.

Tommy was babbling nervously to Nimue. Her eyes canvassed his figure as if scanning it into her data banks for analysis. Son, nephew, brother? Perhaps all three, if the clergy practiced inbreeding (Jack had heard rumors). In any case, Tommy Eichmann's assignment here was clearly nepotism.

Jack interrupted Tommy. "You can see her?" he said, pointing to Nimue.

"I sure can!"

"That's funny, because the Boss—your dad?—says she doesn't exist."

"Huh. That is funny!"

"Yeah. So maybe you could tell the Boss—your uncle?—that I wasn't lying. That I should keep my job and not be tortured."

"Hmm. Maybe we should just do what the Boss says."

"But the planet is at risk. Wouldn't the Boss—your brother?—want to know that?"

"If the planet were at risk, I think the Boss would already know."

Jack wanted to crush Tommy's skull. He had the muscle to do it. The collapsing bone would make a pleasurable sound, the brains would squish sensually through his fingers, and it would perhaps be exciting enough to make him ejaculate in his pants.

He looked at Nimue. Her exposed genitals were likely to be more persuasive than anything Jack could say. "Will you please tell him about the lunatic?"

"What lunatic?"

"The lunatic who wants to kill us. Who lives in a cave full of bones somewhere on this planet and is a threat to all life."

"Oh. Right." She looked at Tommy. "There is a lunatic who lives in a cave full of bones somewhere on this planet and is a threat to all life."

"Wow! That sounds serious! I need to tell the Boss about this!"

Tommy looked at the sun and shouted: "Anilingus to Vatican! Anilingus to Vatican! Come in, Vatican! Do you copy?" He formed a megaphone with his hands and repeated the message. He clearly did not understand the concept of brainwave communication.

Vocalized or not, the thought went unheard. Tommy tried for ten minutes, not wanting to admit defeat. When he finally gave up, he looked sheepishly at Nimue and said, "Must be some atmospheric interference. This happens all the time."

"No it doesn't," Jack said. "But something *is* broken here. That much is clear."

Jack thought he saw Nimue's lips cut to that single-frame grin of hers.

He gave Tommy a tour of the supply closet. A rickety golf cart helped them traverse the long corridors. Like everything else, the golf cart had passed to Jack from his predecessor. Its dash was awash in old magazine clippings—mostly pornographic, mostly tentacles and rape. Jack had let the clippings stay. They were decorative and interesting.

Every cell block of the old prison held its own type of custodial equipment. Jack had just finished showing Cell Block Alpha (Spray Bottles and Aerosol Cans) and was entering Cell Block Beta (Things with Long Handles). The cells here were gargantuan, as if they had been built to jail some race of monsters. Seeing them, Tommy muttered a prayer against the Old Eon. Jack suppressed a grin.

On the long passage between two wings, Tommy

broke off whistling to say to Jack: "So, does Nimue have a boyfriend?"

Jack felt his guts squirm. The sickness of that morning had tapered off as the day progressed, but random waves of it still surged over him. Each wave brought the memory of a powerful tongue laying claim to his anus. He wondered if that tongue would want to enter him again, and if *he* was Nimue's boyfriend.

"I don't know," he answered.

Tommy seemed please. "Tell me about her."

"She came out of the water. She seems to know a lot about mythological beasts. She can fly. I think she has a venereal disease."

"She sounds amazing!"

Jack studied the pudgy man in the passenger seat. He had a vision of Tommy and Nimue rolling on broken eggs in the chicken coop.

He blurted out, "I think she's married." She had told him that; he remembered now. She was Roman Catholic; she was married, with two children (a boy and a girl); and she had ridden a unicorn away from a pond of holy water that had rescued her from death.

"Married?" Tommy's face fell. Then it rose. "Well, that doesn't mean she can't also have a boyfriend!"

"She definitely has a venereal disease."

Tommy didn't know what a venereal disease was.

"Also, she is like a black widow and follows sex with death."

Tommy didn't know what death was. He had heard that it was bad, but that was all.

"Just stay the fuck away from her," Jack said at last. He couldn't shake the vision of Tommy and Nimue locked head-to-ass like copulating earthworms. "Forget her."

But Tommy seemed not to hear. His attention flitted away, and the conversation ended. They entered Cell Block Mu (Ladders Missing One Rung). Jack felt sick.

THIRD SHIFT

"Welcome home, darlings!"

Nimue came out of the trailer to meet them. She was drying her hands on a kitchen towel—as if she'd just been doing dishes—and over her nakedness she wore a matronly apron—as if she'd just been cooking a turkey dinner. The towel and apron matched, both gaudy with cartoon hearts. Jack recognized them from the supply closet.

She rubbed his belly—as if he were pregnant. "How are you feeling?"

"A little better." He indicated her apron. "What's this?"

She didn't answer, peeling off toward Tommy. She patted him on the head. "How was your first day at work, sweetie?" She pressed in with the hearts on her apron.

He blushed. "Oh, just orientation! Jack showed me the supply closet. It's big!"

"We start real work tomorrow," Jack added. He sidled closer, fighting the urge to wedge between them and throw Tommy back twenty feet. "The maniac is still out there. We might die. We might suddenly be decapitated while polishing grains of sand."

"I am going hunting tomorrow," said Nimue. "Soon we will not have to worry about the maniac. In the meantime, it is very important that you do not die; maybe you should stay home tomorrow." She gave his belly another preggers-like rub. "Take a sick day."

"I have to show up for work. Very bad things might happen if I don't. Bishop Eichmann might bypass the Inquisitional Board and send me straight to Hell."

"I'm sure Tommy could talk to the Bishop." She pressed

40

closer to Tommy and caressed his earlobe. The more Jack observed her, the more he noticed how premeditated was her every gesture. How mocking and arrogant. How persuasive. She purred to Tommy, "You have some influence with the Vatican, yes?"

He blushed deeper.

"No," Jack said. "I can't ditch work. I don't want to go to Hell."

They had eggs for supper. Nimue played mother, cracking the eggs into their mouths, making sure they ate well. She rubbed Jack's belly repeatedly. She flirted with Tommy repeatedly. They ate an extravagant amount of eggs; Cleopatra, in amorous tribute to Nimue, had laid twice her usual count, and they were triply delicious.

After dinner, Nimue removed her apron and gave them breast milk for dessert. She made Jack drink from the right nipple, saying, "It is specially formulated for you." Tommy took the left. She cradled their heads.

The milk tasted like honey and sausage.

Jack felt lost in numbness.

A swarm of cupids emerged from Nimue's vagina. The mutant bees ganged up on Tommy, assailing him with their penis-stingers. He groaned around the breast in his mouth. The cupids finished and returned to Nimue's vagina.

Tommy howled as the cupid juice flowed through him.

Fingers of sleep curled into Jack. He fell away from Nimue's milk and lay with eyes half lidded. The world faded in and out, a fog through which two nudes writhed. He saw a pig hand clawing a gorgeous butt cheek. He saw a hairless goddess unreeling lengths of tongue into the anus of a repulsive man-child.

He saw eggs.

41

WEDNESDAY

FIRST SHIFT

Jack awoke to the sound of a toilet being destroyed.

Literally, destroyed. Tommy gripped the sides of the bowl, his body lifting off the seat with each propulsive blast of pandemonium from between his butt cheeks. The porcelain was cracked and crumbling from the repeated shock. The toilet shook like an animal in the throes of death. Jack pitied it.

Tommy looked confused and miserable. Seeing his plight, Jack felt his own bowels begin to turn. He shushed them. He waited until Tommy was done—a long wait—then said: "I told you she had a venereal disease."

Tommy whimpered.

Nimue came in with an armful of eggs for breakfast. She was sunshine and smiles. Her smiles did nothing to change the impression she gave Jack. It did not seem to matter where she swung to on the spectrum of emotiveness; there remained behind her face an immutable blankness.

Jack kept quiet. He played and replayed the memory of last night, of Nimue drugging him with her milk so that she and Tommy could copulate. His brain showed him looped footage of Tommy and Nimue doing it. He tried to overwrite the footage with fantasies of killing Tommy and subjecting Nimue to his sexual will forever. His brain would not comply.

Quietly, he snuck away to vomit.

When he came back, Nimue rubbed his belly. Tommy

seemed to feel better after eating some eggs. Jack looked at him and said, "Get ready for work."

"Hold on," Nimue said.

She grabbed both of their penises and tugged. Jack gasped at the quickness with which he ejaculated. Nimue drew his semen through the fabric of his pants and into her hand. She did the same with Tommy, then rubbed the two handfuls of semen onto her bald head. Her scalp absorbed the pearly slime.

She said, "Now I will be able to monitor your brainwaves while you work. If you insist on going out, I need a way to know that you are safe. I have collected enough gametes to be able to keep watch all day, but you must maintain an erection in order to transmit the signal."

"I don't think that will be a problem," Jack said, tracking the vulturine movement of a cupid overhead. Tommy saw the cupid and groaned. His bowels groaned with him.

Suddenly it was time to go to work.

They clocked in. They waited. Nothing happened. Jack didn't know what to expect. Some communication from Bishop Eichmann, maybe. But there was only that same inexplicable silence on the line. Tommy shouted at the sun. Jack had no idea what was going on—no idea if the Vatican was watching or not… if he was going to die that day or not… if Nimue was his girlfriend or not… if Tommy was Bishop Eichmann or not. He thought about his fear of being sent to Hell, and he wondered if he was already there.

The truck he'd lost in Monday's attack was only one of a fleet. He and Tommy rolled out now in another just like it. Tommy had changed into a pair of blue coveralls. He whistled as they drove out through the hills, away from the janitor's station.

Their first stop was Boogie Wonderland.

Jack worked as if he were alone. He made sure Tommy

was watching, but that was it. The robust flesh of the mushroom forest surrounded him with warmth, and he tried to lose himself in the meditative focus of his janitorial practice. He could not make himself forget that Nimue was monitoring his brainwaves, and he kept unintentionally firing thoughts at her.

I LOVE YOU I LOVE YOU I LOVE YOU.

He wiped dust from the purple cap of a mushroom.

DID HIS ASSHOLE TASTE GOOD?

He strained a piece of litter from a pool of blue goo.

EXCALIBUR EXCALIBUR EXCALIBUR.

Tommy sporadically stopped whistling as bouts of nausea overtook him. Jack worked through his own bouts. He tried to be in the moment; it occurred to him that this was the last time he was likely to be here in Boogie Wonderland. He silently said goodbye to each fungal flower as he washed it.

Often he thought he heard the chop of helicopter blades, but then the sound would vanish. He considered asking Tommy if he heard it. But he didn't want to talk to Tommy.

They finished Boogie Wonderland. Next came the Vast Emptiness.

Some people got off on desolation, and the Vast Emptiness was for them. It was a desert of endless dunes, nothing but bone-white sand as far as the eye could see. The people who made their orgies here sought a world narrowed in focus—for them, there should exist only the scorching sun above, the cutting sands below, and the fetid rectum before them... all the remainder of space-time jettisoned...

Jack only cleaned the Vast Emptiness during Lent. Management at the Vatican were in agreement with this. There was no telling what the desolate ones would do if any outside agent (especially a janitor in lace underwear) pierced their vacuum in mid-rite. And because there was absolutely nothing here but trillions of grains of sand, it was able to pass with being cleaned only once a year. Jack was grateful for that. He sometimes had nightmares about the place.

He started polishing grains of sand.

Tommy watched, seeing how it was done, then started to help. He was no longer whistling. He looked out over the Vast Emptiness and said, "I'm depressed."

Jack said, "Get used to it."

Tommy cleaned sand. His pig hand made it difficult. "I think I am in love with Nimue," he said. "And I think she is in love with me."

Jack said nothing.

"All day I have been hearing a voice sing inside of me. Is that love?"

Jack said nothing.

"I mean there is literally, not figuratively, a voice singing inside of me. In my anus, to be specific. Is that love?"

Jack said, "I don't know what love is."

"The voice is child-like and is singing old tacky pop songs in a sense of irony."

"That doesn't sound like love to me."

Tommy seemed to think about it. Maybe he was listening inward to the pop songs in his colon. Probably he was, because after two to three minutes—pop song length—he smiled decisively and said, "Yep, I am definitely in love!"

Jack could take no more.

He dropped the grain of sand he had been polishing. He faced Tommy and poked a finger at his chest. "I was here first!" he shouted. "I saw her first!"

Tommy looked thunderstruck. "You have feelings for her?"

"YES!" he admitted, to himself and everyone.

"Jack, I had no idea." Tommy gazed away into the desert. "Can we share her?"

"My male possessiveness would never allow such a thing," Jack said, and punched Tommy in the face.

Tommy fell. His nose gushed blood. The blood hit the sand and sizzled in the sun.

"Look at you!" Jack screamed, kicking sand at him. "You're not fit to be a janitor! You think you have what it takes? You have no idea! I am the invisible force that preserves this world, the eternal guardian of order in this hotbed of entropy. You think you can be me?"

Tommy was trying to push the blood back up his nose.

"You only got this job because you're the Boss's son slash nephew slash brother! Your presence here is the symptom of a corrupt system."

Jack felt sick. He listened to Tommy whimper. He heard another sound, barely audible, and listened closer.

It was "Earth Angel"—the 1950s hit—as sung by a child-like voice within Tommy's anus. Jack stood there and listened to the rest of the song, falling out of love with the world. He thought about Hell. Tommy bled in the sand. The sun persisted, quiet and cruel.

Hell was an empty threat, Jack decided.

He said, "I quit."

He walked away into the heart of the Vast Emptiness.

SECOND SHIFT

Jack was in Hell.

Every grain of sand was a damned soul. The sun was Satan, space-time was the Lake of Fire, and gravity was—well, gravity. Jack was in the state of mind called Hell, and Hell was in the state of mind called Jack.

He wandered for hours. He was not lost—he could never get lost on this planet whose every pebble and blade of grass he knew—but he was estranged. He knew exactly where he was, but where he was was nowhere.

His random walk brought him to the geometric center of the desert. He sat down. Excalibur stood perpendicular to the planes of planet and sky. Jack reached inside his coveralls and gripped the antenna by its base. He wondered if he had the strength to snap it off, if doing so would deafen Nimue with a sudden blast of dead-air static.

Instead of snapping it off, he masturbated.

Somehow he had gone seven years without doing this. As the janitor of Planet Anilingus, he had not been permitted to masturbate. Doing so now was an astounding experience. He stripped nude. His discarded coveralls vanished into the sand. He spat a stream of semen at the sun. He rested briefly, then spat again.

Excalibur stayed rigid; a cupid had stung Jack that morning, and he was still riding the wave. He rolled onto his belly, burying Excalibur in the sand. He humped the planet. He wanted to die, so he buried his head in the sand to asphyxiate himself. He became aware again of the sand as a particulate mass of damned souls. He humped the damned

48

souls and breathed them in. As he passed out from lack of oxygen, he ejaculated one last time, into the sand.

Hands gripped him. He returned to dim consciousness with the thought that the Devil had hold of him. He was not alarmed. He was ready to meet someone new.

The Devil lifted Jack out of the sand, from planetary darkness into light.

It was not the Devil. Jack had sand in his eyes, sand in his lungs, but even through the burning and the coughing he could see that his rescuer was man, not demon. The man could be a demon in disguise, of course, but that was true of everything.

Jack recovered his senses. He remembered that he was naked and that the sand had swallowed his coveralls. As a certain stench reached his nostrils, he saw that he had lost control of his bowels. He was still ill with whatever he'd contracted from Nimue, and the stuff that had spewed out of him was a sickening gruel.

He looked at the man who had thwarted his suicide. "Who are you?"

"My name is Virgil." He was dressed as a soldier, laden with esoteric gear. "We met once already. I fired a rocket in your general direction. Several rockets, actually."

The Devil.

Jack said, "Are you going to kill me?"

"No."

"I wouldn't mind if you did. It would save me a lot of trouble."

"I'm not here to kill you. I'm here to help you."

"You could help me by killing me."

"Perhaps." Virgil reached among his gear and came up with a canteen. He unscrewed the lid and tipped cool water into Jack's mouth. "Or, I could offer you some hope. I could help you understand what has happened to your world."

"Yeah?" Jack surveyed the Vast Emptiness. "What *has* happened to my world?"

"A witch was born."

Virgil held up a gloved hand. He peeled off the glove to display his palm. A tattooed mandala of white curves blazed there.

"See this?" he said. "The symbol of my order. The Knights of the Zygote."

"Never heard of them."

"No one has. We are of the Shadow Vatican—which is to say, the true Vatican—and we answer only to the Shadow Pope—which is to say, the true Pope. We are the inner meaning of the Church. We are the flaming sword of God."

"And I'm a janitor."

"Please do not interrupt my exposition." Virgil put his glove back on. He lifted his shirt. Centered on his navel was another tattooed glyph. "The Seal of Solomon," he called it. "Fire and water." He dropped his shirt. "It is a pity that we have not the time to delve into the fullness of things. I should like to play Metatron. But urgency forces my hand, and we must assume the frame of reference that is most expedient—which is to say, the merely scientific.

"This world has given birth." He reached down and patted the vast flank of Anilingus. "Planets are bodies. Bodies are nodes of negative entropy. All bodies have an organizing force—a morphic field—guiding them toward ever higher states of order. This force begets the stars; then, from the raw material of the stars, it begets the planets; then, from the raw material of the planets, it begets living organisms. From simple organisms it begets more complex ones. Under the influence of a morphic field, any raw material can develop into complex life.

"A morphic field itself is a kind of entity—noncorporeal, beyond spatiotemporal understanding. There are many such entities, all vying for control of the raw material of physics. One morphic field in particular has gained dominion over the plane we inhabit. This field is that entity you call God."

"But I thought God was an old man somewhat reminiscent of my grandfather."

"Again, please do not interrupt my exposition. No, God is not an old man somewhat reminiscent of your grandfather. There is no such God as that; there is only the morphic field that has channeled swirling hydrogen into sexually reproducing humans.

"The sexually reproducing human is the vanguard of God's project. This project is mathematically continuous and irreversible; it progresses only forward, and forward only as a modulation of the present state. Therefore, all further development must proceed from the sexually reproducing human—which is to say, from the fusion of gametes produced in the human ovary and the human testicle.

"But it happens that other morphic fields—other gods—attempt to derail the continuity of this progression—to usurp the modulating force of God and introduce their own designs upon this plane. These designs do not proceed logically from the present state; they are new directions. They need not take as their starting point the fusion of ovarian and testicular gametes. They can begin anew, discontinuous as they please.

"Anilingus has slipped into the influence of a divergent field. A form of complex life has been born here, a form that does not proceed from the established generative procedure. This life form arises from the fusion of gametes produced in the human mouth and the human anus.

"Which is to say, the act of anilingus has become procreative."

In Jack's bowels, something kicked.

"The Zygotic Knights are stewards of the dominant morphic field called God. We police the trajectory of this plane and prune all movement contrary to the field. In a sense, we *are* the field. We are God."

Jack said, "Hi, God. It's nice to meet you, I guess." He considered burying his head in the sand again. His guts rumbled. "I'm pregnant, aren't I? That's what you're saying."

"Yes. You are gestating a witch in your lower intestines."

Jack did not know what a witch was.

Virgil said, "A witch is any life form arising from a morphic field other than God. The Knights of the Zygote hunt and kill witches."

"So you want to give me an abortion?"

"We must kill the babe, yes, but that is not our first priority. More pressing than the unborn witch is the one already loose on this planet. The witch who impregnated you."

"Nimue."

"Whatever it calls itself. This witch sprung from an act of anilingus. It is the first of its kind. Its parents were two insignificant businessmen who coupled at random. It is inevitable that competing morphic fields will sporadically make inroads into this plane, and that is what happened upon that random coupling. There was nothing special about the coupling, nothing to distinguish it from the other thousand instances of ass-licking going on nearby. It was simply time for the inevitable to occur. We call it Immaculate Conception."

"Conception involving tongues and anuses doesn't sound very 'immaculate' to me." Jack recalled his night in the chicken coop with Nimue and Cleopatra. He wondered if he would have still had sex with Nimue, knowing she was a witch born of mouth and ass. He had certainly had sex with Cleopatra, knowing she was a chicken. This new truth about Nimue did not change his feelings. "She told me she was a married Roman Catholic with two children."

"The witch is a liar. What else did it tell you?"

"That you were a psychotic crucifix salesman who tried to kill her, that a miracle of holy water saved her from death, that she rode a unicorn. What is a unicorn?"

"Another type of witch. One we exterminated long ago."

Virgil looked at the sun. He looked at the sand. He looked at Jack. "The witch you call Nimue is a highly advanced form of life. More advanced than us. It is inventive, persuasive, and unpredictable. Supernatural, even. If it were to gain dominion here, the morphic field behind it would assume control of our plane and abort God's design. It would be an abomination. We must exterminate the witch."

"But I love her—I think."

"The witch has you enchanted. You are the mother of its progeny. When you deliver, the newborn witch will eat you alive, just as Nimue did to that first unsuspecting mother."

Jack felt sick—whether from the prospect of death, of life, of love, or of loss, he did not know. "When do I give birth?"

Virgil bent an ear to Jack's stomach. He reached around to palpate Jack's sphincter, little finger diving quickly inside. Examination finished, he faced Jack and said, "Three days. You have three days until the witch is born from your rectum and eats you alive."

THIRD SHIFT

Virgil seemed to know the planet as well as Jack. He walked ahead, as if leading, and Jack followed, as if following. Jack had made a token search for his coveralls before they left, but the sands of the Vast Emptiness were jealous of their spoils, and Jack was still naked. Despite his buff physique, he did not feel confident being nude.

"We are nearing the edge of the desert," Virgil said. He stopped, rooted through his gear, and came up with a length of cord, which he handed to Jack. "You must bind your penis."

"What?" Jack took the cord, looked at it.

"Tie your penis to your leg. We will soon be prey again to the sting of *Apis cupidus*. This desert biome is useful as a base of operations because, being devoid of everything, it is also devoid of the cupid. It is the only place on the planet where it is possible to escape having a nearly constant erection, and thus to escape carrying the antenna that broadcasts our thoughts to the witch."

"She can scan your brainwaves too? How did she get your semen?"

"During our first confrontation, the witch absconded with one of my testicles. Tore it right from my sac. She has kept it alive in her own body, giving her endless access to my gametes, and thus to my mind. However, she still needs an unimpeded signal from an operational antenna, and I have bested her in this by keeping my erection tied down—as you now must do."

Jack looked at the cord again, and at his naked penis. It was flaccid, had been since his last spurt into the sand. Virgil was right; this was the only place where prolonged respite from arousal was possible. "So tying my penis to my leg is supposed to, what, impede the signal?"

"Exactly."

Jack tied his penis to his leg.

They crossed out of the Vast Emptiness and into Boogie Wonderland. A cupid found Jack almost immediately. He watched his penis grow erect, straining against its bonds. It hurt. He listened for the sound of helicopter blades. He heard moss growing, frogs croaking in the bogs of Boogie Wonderland, but that was it.

He found the place where he and Tommy had left the truck. The truck was gone. Tommy might have driven it back to the janitor's station, or some bog monster might have swallowed it. There were no tracks, no sign of Tommy.

More curious than concerned, Jack asked Virgil, "Do you know where Tommy went? The guy I was training— short, pudgy, annoying."

"I don't know. I left him to follow you."

Jack shivered as a frog in the bog swallowed a razor and sang. He shivered as a bat and a rat (mechanical and animal, respectively) squeaked in unison. He shivered, and his pregnant rectum groaned, and a diarrheal anvil dropped on his head.

He shat out a frog, a bat, and a rat.

"Aghhhhh!" he screamed, feeling the creatures explode from his rectum, then watching them hop, flap, and scuttle away into the twilight.

Virgil seemed unalarmed. He pulled a tiny knife from somewhere and threw it at the bat. The bat went down, skewered, and Virgil retrieved it. He inspected his kill, turning the knife for different angles. The bat's fur was matted with Jack's feces, more feces caked among the spinning cogs visible through an open panel on its belly.

"The pregnancy is advancing," Virgil said. "Your bowels are becoming subject to exotic dimensions of nausea." He indicated the bat. "This kind of thing is going to start happening more often." He flicked the knife to dislodge the bat from it, folded the knife away, and walked on as if nothing had happened.

"Hold on," Jack said. "Get this witch child out of me. Before we go any further. I don't want to be subject to exotic dimensions of nausea. I don't want creepy things to randomly fly out of my ass. And, despite my recent attempted suicide and general ambivalence regarding whether I live or die, I don't particularly want to be eaten alive anytime soon. I want an abortion."

"The adult witch is our primary target. Then we deal with the babe."

"Why does it have to wait? Can't you just stick a coat hanger up my ass and be done with it?"

"I'm afraid a coat hanger up the ass won't be enough. The unborn witch is impervious to any assault we could make. In its incipient state, it is still only an enfolded manifestation of a morphic field; it does not yet have full spatiotemporal existence. Therefore, it is beyond our reach. It must first finish taking form."

An aftershock of nausea hit Jack. He braced himself for another parade of creatures out of his ass, but instead there was only a brief spell of polka music that echoed through his colon and faded sharply. "You mean I have to actually carry this thing to term? What if it eats me before we get a chance to kill it?"

"We will have to act quickly. Upon birth, the larval witch almost instantly develops into mature form, but during those first few moments it is vulnerable. That is when we strike."

"You better be ready."

"I am the flaming sword of God. I am always ready."

Boogie Wonderland segued into a field of funhouse paraphernalia: distorted mirrors, wobbly walls, stretches of floor where circular platforms spun at odds with each other. Jack hated the place; it made him queasy. It had no real name, referenced in discourse only by a wild eruption of laughter. For example: "Where were you?" "Oh, I was in *Ha ha ha ha ha!*"

A distorted mirror gave Jack a fat belly. A preggers belly. He looked at the spinning floor, remembering it filled with giggling men and women who licked ass all around him as he stumbled through the funhouse trying to clean.

They were nearing the janitor's station. Virgil seemed to have some plan of action in mind, but he wasn't sharing it; he simply steamed ahead, purpose-driven, and Jack tried to keep up. The funhouse amplified his nausea; crossing a teeter-totter hallway, he vomited up part of a snapped bicycle chain.

"This place is impossible," he said.

"We could travel more efficiently on the main highway," Virgil said, "but at the sacrifice of stealth. If we hope to catch the witch unawares, we must maintain our cover."

They entered a hall of mirrors. Jack said, "You seem to know this planet as well as I do."

"I know it better than you do."

Jack walked through a crowd of himself.

They mounted the low hills that masked the janitor's station. Below, Jack saw the small bur of aluminum that was his trailer. He looked for a truck parked anywhere near— evidence that Tommy had driven himself home. He did not see it.

It was open land between here and the complex, nothing to conceal their crossing. Virgil crouched, unpacking one of his bags of gear. He unfolded a large overgarment covered in leaves and grass. "A ghillie suit," he called it. "Camouflage."

He had only one.

"Climb on top of me," he told Jack.

Jack climbed on top of him, piggyback style. Virgil donned the ghillie suit, wearing it over the both of them. He stretched flat on the ground and started to crawl.

They advanced at an imperceptible pace; anyone looking would not have seen anything but an oddly hunched piece of land. It was hot inside the suit of foliage. Jack—naked, penis strapped to leg, hugged piggyback to the creeping sword of God—was uncomfortable.

It took an hour to come within range of the complex. When they did, Virgil peeked out of the ghillie suit. He gazed intently at Jack's trailer, waiting for some sign of his prey.

"She might not be here," Jack whispered.

Virgil hushed him.

They heard helicopter blades.

Nimue exploded through the roof of the trailer, her blades ripping a jagged hole in the aluminum. Virgil rose, throwing off the ghillie suit (Jack with it) and raising a handheld rocket launcher. He spat a load of fire at the escaping witch.

Jack's trailer disappeared into a giant pumpkin of flame.

Nimue shot upward, barely outrunning the expanding edge of the explosion. She caught sight of Jack and Virgil. At this distance her features were indistinct, but it seemed that she smiled at them... amused, perhaps, to see Jack and Virgil—the "depraved maniac"—together, and to see the obvious implication of this: that Jack now knew the truth of her.

So smiling, she fled in the direction of the supply closet slash old prison. The drone of her blades faded until it vanished beneath the roar of the burning trailer. In frustration, Virgil fired another rocket after her—but she was gone, swallowed into the dusk.

THURSDAY

FIRST SHIFT

Jack awoke on the charred remains of his cot. He had a headache. He rubbed his temple, still had a headache. Morning sun streamed in through a dozen places in the crispy husk of the trailer. The air was thick with cupids.

Jack shifted and found himself facing Virgil. The man sat full-lotus on the floor, whirlwinds of ash about his knees. His eyes, wide and fixed, were those of a man who had not slept (or blinked, even) all night.

Jack could think of nothing to say. His penis hurt. Excalibur was bound extra tightly to his leg, the cords cutting into him. Virgil thought that he had been bound too loosely the previous night, and that this was in part responsible for tipping off Nimue to their presence.

The witch hunter inhaled deeply and, perhaps for the first time in hours, blinked. Jack thought he saw a nictitating membrane somewhere in that blink.

"How do you feel?" Virgil said.

"Better." Shortly after their failed attack, Jack had plummeted into nausea and had started vomiting reels of celluloid. He blacked out, or passed out, or a verse-chorus-verse of both. He thought he remembered watching Virgil extinguish the flaming trailer with something that looked like a seltzer bottle. This was mixed with dreams of John Wayne as Jesus Christ in a Western retelling of the crucifixion.

Jack rolled out of his cot. He took some eggs from the refrigerator. They had cooked in the fire, and he ate them like raw potatoes.

There was no sign of Cleopatra. Perhaps she was somewhere among the cinders, dead, fried extra crispy.

He kicked through a pile of the charred detritus that coated the floor. There, amid blackened copies of *Body and Blood* and *TV Guide*, he found, miraculously untouched, a pair of lace underwear and a bowtie. Tired of being naked, he donned the underwear. Then he eyed the bowtie. The underwear sufficed to cover his nudity; he didn't need the bowtie.

He put it on anyway.

Dressed, he stared through a hole in the wall, its fire-blackened edges framing a portion of the black fortress that loomed up behind the trailer. Nimue had fled out over that sprawl, and Jack imagined she was still there, somewhere among the towers and wings.

Virgil said, "The witch dies today."

Suddenly it was time to go to work.

Jack did not look at the sun to clock in. He figured his days of clocking in were over.

Bishop Eichmann's head popped out of the ground.

Jack had never seen the man look so furious, so close to myocardial infarction. The stiff bristles of his Hitler mustache were standing on end.

Jack stood over the transubstantiated head. It did not even cross his mind to lower himself level with the head. Jack waited for the Boss to speak, and the Boss waited for Jack to lie on the ground. The longer he waited, the redder he grew. Finally, seeing that Jack would not grovel, he caved.

"You're going to burn in Hell, Jack!"

Jack said, "I no longer know what that means." He wondered if Virgil could explain Hell in terms of his "morphic fields"—probably Virgil could explain everything. "There is a lot going on that you're unaware of, Bishop. I think you're in over your head."

The Bishop screamed, "Where the hell is my Tommy?"

"He is in danger. Tommy—your son?—went missing

yesterday. I don't know where he is now. I think a witch might have kidnapped him."

The Bishop screamed, "What did you do to my Tommy? You fell off the map again yesterday, and now here you are, and my Tommy is missing!"

"We will find him."

"*We?*"

Just then Virgil came out of the trailer, where he had been finishing some last minute yoga movements.

The Bishop screamed, "Who the hell is that?"

Virgil looked down at the head of dirt and grass. "I am the flaming sword of God. I am the inner meaning of the faith you pretend, Bishop."

Bishop Eichmann had a heart attack. The pain jiggled through his transubstantiated face. Wherever his actual body was, an assistant came with a syringe and dealt with the crisis. The Bishop rebounded with the ease of one accustomed to this routine. He looked calmly at Jack and Virgil and said, "I want a full explanation in five hundred words or less."

"No," Virgil said.

"That's it," said the Bishop. "I'm coming down there. And I'm bringing reinforcements."

"I urge you not to do that," Virgil said.

Jack said, "We will find your nephew. We'll find Tommy."

"Yes," Virgil agreed. "We must, for he is also gestating a witch."

Jack had not realized this. It seemed obvious now, considering the symptoms Tommy had after his night with Nimue. A cold front of jealousy hit Jack. He had felt a strange sense of prestige at being a mother, and now he had to share that title.

Yet, as nausea struck anew and gold coins slot-machined out of his ass, he wondered why he would ever be jealous of such a thing.

The Bishop stared. "Are you shitting coins, Jack?"

Jack regained composure long enough to say, "Yes." The coins overflowed from his underwear like too many fish in a net, forming a pile at his feet.

"I'm coming down there," the Bishop said again. "With a legion of soldiers. You are to ready a vessel for me, and one hundred vessels for my men."

"It will take a long time to slaughter one hundred and one pigs."

"You have until tomorrow morning."

"I could be using that time to look for your brother."

"Ready the vessels. I will be monitoring you; do not disobey my edict."

The Bishop's head turned back into dirt and grass.

"Jackass," Virgil said. "He knows nothing. He is a puppet. Forget him; our mission supersedes all. Come." He started toward the cyclopean door of the supply closet. "Do not worry about the Bishop monitoring you. The witch has a blockade on transmissions to and from this planet. It falters periodically—I don't know why—and a transmission gets through, as you just saw; but otherwise we are totally locked down."

"I've noticed," Jack said, remembering his frustrated attempts at contact.

"It has complicated my job severely. No assistance from HQ, no intel. I am a lone agent, disconnected. We have not done a job like this in centuries. In a sense, the witch has flung this planet into the past."

They stood before the entrance to the supply closet slash old prison. The building had straddled that dichotomy as long as Jack had known it, but now it tipped decidedly in one direction, and he saw only the prison. The building that had been his supply closet was gone, and here things were not merely stored, merely placed, but jailed. What was jailed was the stuff of Jack's life—the implements and paraphernalia of his function, the cloud of his technological extensions. What was jailed was Jack.

The Old Eon had returned, and Anilingus was Panopticon 4 again.

Jack took a final glance at the sun, then followed Virgil through the yawning entrance, into the bowels of the prison planet.

SECOND SHIFT

Jack suggested traveling by golf cart, but Virgil insisted on moving more stealthily.

This meant: ghillie suit.

Jack said, "I don't think a suit of grass and leaves will work indoors."

Virgil sifted through his gear. He found what he was looking for, and it was not a suit of grass and leaves. Apparently he had more than one type of ghillie suit; this one was covered in bricks, floor tiles, dust bunnies, rags—all the "foliage" of an indoor environment.

"Climb on top of me," Virgil said.

And then they were crawling in tandem beneath the indoor ghillie suit.

It took an hour just to make it through Cell Block Alpha (Spray Bottles and Aerosol Cans). Jack was sweating beneath the suit of habitational foliage. His lace underwear was soaked, and his bowtie was choking him. Excalibur, bound, pressed close to the gear-laden space between Virgil's buttocks. A clock ticked somewhere among all the gear, and Jack listened, aware that each tick brought him closer to the matricidal hunger of his witchy offspring.

An interminable time later, they reached Cell Block Delta (Vacuum Cleaners of Indeterminate Sucking Power), and fresh nausea gripped Jack.

He started to float away.

Jack had never before been lighter than air. The experience was astounding. An invisible force lifted him. He felt like oil in water. The knowledge struck him that air *was* water, and that he was an underwater creature—some kind of crab scuttling its life away across an ocean floor. And now the ocean of air was ejecting him, squeezing him up into the next sphere of density.

Into outer space?

The ceiling would stop him—but what if the ceiling was made of fog?

"Help!" He dug his hands into the gear on Virgil's back, holding on. His lower body kept rising, lifting the ghillie suit with it. He lost his grip, and the air took him.

Virgil jumped up, pulling from his gear an authentic Old West lasso. He twirled the lasso above his head and let the looped end sail. It caught Jack around the waist. Virgil yanked his end of the lasso, tightening the loop around Jack.

Jack shat crucifixes (chintzy plastic ones) as the witch hunter reeled him in. Afloat and on a line, Jack felt like a balloon, like a kite. The crucifixes overflowed from his lace underwear and rained down to the floor.

Virgil drew in the Jack-balloon. He tied the line to the bars of a nearby cell. He said, "Your condition is progressing more rapidly than I anticipated."

Jack was too incapacitated to reply. He hallucinated oncoming headlights, flinched from them, woke up in the middle of surgery, was put back under.

Virgil said, "You might start going into labor soon." He pulled from his gear a giant syringe. "This will counteract the symptoms. It will slow the gestating witch." He plunged the syringe into the base of Jack's spine.

Crackling warmth flooded Jack. It was like an intravenous injection of pop rocks and photons. He stopped seeing headlights, stopped shitting crucifixes. He sank slowly out of the air. His feet touched down, and Virgil untied him.

"What was that?" he said, indicating the syringe.

Virgil placed the syringe in a biohazard bag. "Holy water. A pure distillate of the sovereign morphic field. It will sum with the rogue field, dampening some of its anomalous spikes, modulating it. It will buy us some time."

Jack remembered Nimue's tall tale about the pond, the holy water entering her spinal wound (wound, or natural orifice of her witchy biology?) and infusing her system. The syringe of holy water to his own spine now was like a refrain of that. He mentioned it to Virgil.

Virgil said, "The witch often hides prophecy in its lies. It finds it amusing."

Jack wondered if this meant that he would soon encounter a unicorn. He looked at the suit of bricks, tiles, dust, and rags. "I'm not getting back under that thing."

"You're right. We have less time than I thought. We must sacrifice stealth for speed. Stay low and follow me."

Jack discovered that he was not completely cured of buoyancy. As he walked, each step felt higher, farther, freer than he was accustomed to. It was like walking through a field of lesser gravity. Once adjusted to it, he found it pleasurable.

Virgil led, analyzing the environment according to some arcane science of tracking. He found smears of webbing attached to the walls and insisted that these were left by the witch, although to Jack they looked like common spider webs. He found droppings and insisted that these too were left by the witch, although to Jack they looked like rat turds.

In Cell Block Sigma (Chains), they found a torn pair of blue coveralls. To Jack they looked like Tommy's. He recognized a stain on the collar. Leading away from the coveralls was a trail of gold coins and crucifixes greased with feces.

Tommy was somewhere ahead—captive, naked, and in an advanced stage of pregnancy. And wherever Tommy was, Nimue was likely near.

"We're close," Virgil said.

THIRD SHIFT

"Do I have Satan in my rectum?"

"What?"

"The child in my anus. Is it the Antichrist?"

They were making a brief stop to catch their breath. A jail cell full of gloves offered adequate concealment, and they sat in the back corner, eating MREs that Virgil had pulled from one of his many rucksacks. "We must ingest calories," the witch hunter had said, handing Jack an egg omelet MRE and taking a vegetable lasagna one for himself.

Virgil wiped lasagna juice from his chin. "No, the witch in your anus is not Satan or the Antichrist. There is no Satan, no Antichrist—no God, as a matter of fact. These are terms of convenience borrowed from Church mythology; they are heuristic, not descriptive, terms. They point to patterns, fields of order."

Jack found some candy in his MRE. He smiled.

Virgil continued, "The patterns compete, but not in the sense of an active antagonism. Active antagonism would imply volition, perhaps some level of sentience; the patterns transcend these. Theirs is a mathematical competition—a superimposition of waveforms, chaos equations in summation, basins of attraction emerging."

Jack ate chocolate and said, "I have no education in theology or mathematics. I've been trained as a custodian since birth."

Virgil ate peanut butter. "I have also been trained since birth. I cannot be other than what I am. We are what we are."

Jack looked around the mammoth jail cell. He wondered again what type of monster had once been locked in here.

Now the cell held only gloves, endless heaps of them. Jack sat on a pile of six-fingered ones.

Virgil said, "I serve the pattern I serve because it is part of the pattern I serve that I serve it." He put gum in his mouth, chewed it for twenty seconds, and spat it out. "Are you fed and rested? We must carry on."

They made fantastic progress. Jack's buoyant gait allowed him to keep up with Virgil, and they had a clear trail of Tommy's droppings to follow (the coins and crucifixes gave way to books and dinner plates, which gave way to sewing machines and baby grand pianos; Jack imagined the hell that Tommy's body must be going through, and he gave thanks to the holy water in his veins for saving him from the same—gave thanks, but wondered how much longer it would last).

It dawned on Jack that their hunt was moving in a definite pattern: a spiral tightening toward the center of the prison. At the center was Cell Block Omega (Nothing). Jack, in the course of his work, had found need for almost everything in his stock—even such seemingly useless equipment as what was in Cell Block Lambda (Assorted Infomercial Purchases)—but he had never found need for what was in Cell Block Omega (Nothing). He had never been there.

That was about to change.

They arrived at an enormous staircase spiraling down into the planet. It had not the penitentiary look of the rest of the facilities, resembling instead the central staircase in some palatial mansion. A trail of grand pianos (no longer baby grands, but concert grands) led down the stairs.

A neon sign said: OMEGA.

Jack gazed over the edge of the giant spiral staircase,

trying to see the bottom. There was only darkness down there. A draft rose from far below, warm and sour like the breath of an ogre.

"The descent will take several hours," Virgil said. "Too bad you are not still a balloon, otherwise I would hang on and we could float down."

"I am still a little lighter than air." He bounced on his feet, proving it. "Want to try?"

Virgil started down the stairs.

"Guess not," Jack said to himself, and started after him.

An hour down, there was still no sign of the bottom. The pianos that dotted the stairs had become player pianos, keys ghosting through preprogrammed music. Jack heard as many as three pianos going at once, detuned and dissonant; they all seemed to be playing the chord progression of "Earth Angel"—the 1950s hit—but in differing keys and tempos.

Virgil said, "The pianos will mask the sound of our approach."

"I wish they'd at least play a different song," Jack said.

"No, this is a good song." Virgil closed his eyes and mouthed the words.

They started to encounter other things along with the pianos: antique tractors, outhouses, famous landmarks (the Eiffel Tower, the Statue of Liberty, Stonehenge). As much as he hated the man, Jack felt bad for Tommy.

They stopped to study a strange dropping. It was huge and teetered precariously on the edge of the stairs. Jack at first did not know what he was looking at, but then he realized that it was a conglomeration of all the previous droppings: it was a piano slash tractor slash outhouse slash sailboat slash film crew slash pile of money slash too many things to process. The piano portion was set into the engine compartment of the tractor portion, the black and white keys still rippling their song. The sailboat creaked, prow angled upward as if sinking into the rest of the morass. The whole thing was like a big irregular meteor.

Virgil said, "Your friend is almost out of time."

"He's not really my friend," Jack said. "We just work together."

Virgil checked a timepiece on his wrist, calculating in his head. Jack looked too and saw that it was almost midnight.

Virgil took his Old West lasso, lashed it around Jack's waist, and leapt from the spiraling staircase, out over the abyss. Jack had no time to react. The rope pulled taut and jerked him over the edge, and he and Virgil were falling.

Jack's little bit of buoyancy slowed their fall only slightly. He did not make a very good balloon, still too full of holy water.

Virgil held to the rope of the Jack-balloon. The staircase corkscrewed around them as they fell. Jack heard pianos tinkling beneath the roaring wind of their descent.

Jack wondered if taking a deep breath and holding it would make him more buoyant, more of a balloon. He knew it wouldn't, tried it anyway. He realized they were going to die.

He shouted down to Virgil, "I wish you would have consulted me about this!"

Virgil gazed up at him. "You said you were still lighter than air!"

"I may have overestimated how much lighter!"

The air went right through Jack's lace underwear. He felt the straps around Excalibur loosening. He tried to hold the erection in place, to keep his thoughts from coming open to Nimue. He would not admit to himself that he was on his way to assist in her execution. Did he love her? Virgil said she had him under a spell. It was probably true, but did it matter? He was under the spell he was under because it was part of the spell he was under that he be under it. Isn't that love?

His bowtie started to spin. The air was catching it, turning it like a fan blade. Like a helicopter blade. It spun slowly at first, then quickly, then more quickly, then quickest. Jack tilted his head back to give the tiny propeller room to turn.

The spinning bowtie gave them lift, slowed their fall. They were not going to die.

Virgil hung from his tether, gazing up at the propeller. "Yes, exactly what I thought would happen! You see, we were never in any real danger!"

The witch hunter wiped beads of sweat from his brow.

For the propeller to work, Jack had to maintain an extreme angle in the backward tilt of his head. It hurt, but not as much as the impact from a sky-high freefall would hurt.

Hours passed as Jack and Virgil sank through the air. Still no sign of the bottom. No sign of the top now, either; above and below, the spiral staircase wound out of sight. Jack tried to calculate how far down they were. The calculation kept tangling, fraying. Jack gave it up.

Virgil held his tether, saying nothing. He practiced yoga movements modified to work in midair. All was darkness and soft piano music.

Jack fell asleep.

FRIDAY

FIRST SHIFT

Jack awoke to utter darkness. The flow of air told him he was still falling.

Virgil shouted, "Brace yourself!"

They hit metal. Even with Jack's bowtie-propeller slowing their fall, the impact was bone-rattling. Jack bit his tongue, cracked a tooth, swallowed wrong, sprained his ankle, stubbed his toe. His vision swam with stars, little birdies, cupids.

He felt Virgil's hands on him. "Are you alive?"

"Yes," Jack tried to say, but only moaned.

Virgil lit a torch.

Jack said, "Where did you get a torch?"

From his gear, of course. He held the torch close to the metal floor, inspecting it. It was rust-spotted, banded with thick seams where separate plates met. There was a slight curvature to it. "This appears to be some huge shell or hull," Virgil said.

Jack sat up, shaking the stars and birdies from his head. He ran his hands along the metal shell. He knew the circumference of Anilingus, knew the formula for finding its radius; he was certain they had fallen at least that far. "This," he said, "is the center of the planet. The center of Panopticon 4. This," he banged a fist against the metal, producing a sonorous clang, "is a prison cell."

OMEGA.

Virgil swept his torch in a wide circle, observing the enormity of the hull. "What could have been imprisoned here?"

It was a rhetorical question; he didn't really want to know.

Jack couldn't have told him, anyway. Time had swallowed the Old Eon and its monsters. There were new monsters in the world. Whatever Omega had once held, Jack knew what it held now: Nothing.

But was Nothing a new monster?—or a very old one?—the oldest? Omega might have always jailed this same monster, even through the Old Eon… even before the Old Eon (the Older Eon?)… from one end of time to the other.

"I see the hatch," Virgil said, and started toward it.

Jack might have asked for a moment to prepare himself, but Virgil would have plowed ahead regardless. Anyway, there was really nothing he could do to prepare. Virgil was right to plow ahead. It was the only way to face this.

Virgil turned the wheel that unlocked the hatch. It squealed hideously, scabs of rust coughing out of its joints. He threw open the hatch, and a square beam of whitest light burst forth from within.

The light had the intensity of a mammoth laser; it was opaque, almost a solid object. Virgil's head was in its path. The light decapitated him. His head popped off, twirled upward a short distance, then dropped like a stone through the open hatch, going quietly into the blinding white of Nothing.

Jack screamed, "Aghhhhh!"

But the witch hunter was not dead. His headless body groped through its jumble of gear, pulling from somewhere a spare cranium. Virgil lifted the fresh head to his shoulders and screwed it into place. He blinked, yawned, his face coming alive. It was not the same face as before. He had changed hairstyle, age, ethnicity.

"I have to be more careful," he said, backing away from the beam of light. He looked at Jack. His new face wore sunglasses and had two teardrops tattooed on its left cheek. Its lips were chapped. "Are you ready?"

74

Jack said, "I don't have any spare heads."

"Neither do I, now. This was my last." Virgil approached the light flooding out through the hatch. He passed an arm through the light, and the limb came out unscathed. "It should be safe to enter. The light discharged most of its energy in that one big spurt."

Jack crept toward the opening and peered inside. He saw a white void without dimension. He thought of a perfect and infinite egg.

"Is this Hell?" he said.

Virgil said, "Follow me."

Inside Omega, there was no gravity—or rather, there was the culmination of gravity: the bottom of the gravity well, no further to fall. They floated, two balloons suspended in an invisible gel. An absurdly long rope trailed behind them, leading back to the hatch. It was their Trail of Breadcrumbs, and it was good they had it, for the hatch had vanished in the distance and there would be no other way out of this Witch's Lair. The flat white space had swallowed them whole, and only this fragile umbilicus offered hope of return.

Jack could not tell if they were moving or floating in place. He had never before experienced such a complete cancellation of forces. It was astounding. It was like being born into a new reality. He liked it. Maybe this was Heaven.

An impurity appeared in the void. It grew larger as it approached them, or as they approached it, or as they and it approached each other.

It was an asteroid made of houses and orchestras. One of Tommy's droppings. It spun along some unanalyzable combination of axes, roaring as it passed them, or as they passed it, or as they and it passed each other.

Something caressed Jack's cheek. He brushed at the spot, and his hand came away with threads of gossamer stuck to it. The stuff was weightless, nearly invisible. More strands touched him. He could not brush them all away. Focusing his vision, he saw the ghostly stuff everywhere, razor-thin strands of it woven into a baroque pattern.

It was a web.

The web grew denser. They cut through with machetes.

More asteroids appeared. Their ingredients were breaking down, fragmenting: instead of a whole house, there was a roof shingle, a doorknob, a shutter; instead of a full orchestra, there was a frayed violin bow, a gap-toothed glockenspiel, the jawbone of a first-chair flutist. Soon the huge concretions of matter became nothing more than turds of chance form. They decomposed further, shedding all detail to become generic wads of primordial tissue.

These wads hung tangled in the web, spaced like cystic nodes. As Jack and Virgil penetrated deeper, the nodes bled together with the web, condensing into one substance.

Jack stopped swinging his machete. The condensed substance was too thick. He was immersed in it, as if underwater. It had the consistency of semen, the color of old eyes. It got into his mouth; he could not prevent it. He ate it, breathed it.

It tasted like egg yolk.

They traveled deep into the yolk and found Tommy at its center.

His body hung as if on a cross, nailed to the molecular web of the yolk. He was in a state of semi-consciousness. Jack floated in close and tried to rouse him. He slapped him, kicked him, screamed at him. It was fun, but it didn't do any good.

Jack noticed a disturbance in the yolk around Tommy.

There seemed to be a current here. He moved in closer and discovered its source.

The yolk was emanating from Tommy. It flowed outward from every orifice and pore of his naked body, rippling like the quicksilver stuff of an escaping soul.

Here was the font of the expanding bubble that Jack and Virgil had arrived through. The yolk was the advanced form of Tommy's nauseous secretions.

And they were swimming in it.

Jack felt sick.

Three things happened at once:

Nimue slinked into frame on spider legs.

Tommy awoke screaming.

Jack's boss showed up. With reinforcements.

Jack went from feeling sick, to sicker, to sickest. He wondered what had happened to the peace of his deserted planet. He wished he could be polishing moss in Boogie Wonderland. But his job description had changed. He still thought of himself as a janitor, but the title had taken on new meaning. Entropy had a new face.

Suddenly it was time to go to work.

SECOND SHIFT

Bishop Eichmann was a pig. The hundred soldiers with him—were pigs. Jack had neglected the order to slaughter vessels for the Bishop and his men, and they had unwittingly transubstantiated into live swine. The living flesh resisted their efforts to rework it, human will and pig will at war within a single body. The result was a legion of mutant pig-men.

Bishop Eichmann had a Hitler mustache on his pig face.

He glared at Jack. "Jack!" He saw Tommy. "*Tommy!*" He noticed Nimue. "DEVIL!"

Virgil leaned close to Jack and spoke in a low voice, as if they were a two-man football team huddled up before the final play. "I take the witch. You fend off the Bishop and his men, or else that meddling fool could ruin everything."

"How did he even find us here?"

"Pigs have an excellent sense of smell. Do you know how to use one of these?" He gave Jack a tommy gun with a drum magazine. "Just aim and squeeze the trigger."

Jack examined the tommy gun. He found a Big Gangster Cigar stuffed into the barrel as a complementary addendum. He removed the cigar and clamped it in his teeth, snarling around it. "Let's kill some pigs."

"If anything happens to me—good luck. When that witch child comes out of you, it's going to be hungry."

"I'll be okay. I have nine lives."

"And I have nine million—but only one of them is on this plane. Do not fear death, Jack; it doesn't really exist."

"Does love exist?" He glanced out of the huddle, toward Nimue lurking on her spider legs. She smiled at him.

Virgil said, "Love is witchy." He pulled out a sword. "Time to do God's work."

"No," Jack said, "I'm done working for other people. I work for myself now."

They broke the huddle, shouting in unison: "Break!"

Jack launched himself through the yolk, opening fire on the legion of Vatican pig-men. Cigar in mouth, he swept his tommy gun across the horde. Excalibur had come fully untied from his leg, standing perpendicular now, visible through the sheer lace of his underwear. Jack could not recall the last time a cupid had stung him. He was freely, willfully erect. Excalibur was his.

His cigar, unlit till now, ignited spontaneously. He had to laugh.

Bishop Eichmann detached from the throng, hurtling himself toward Tommy, who had not stopped screaming since he awoke. Jack gave the army of pig-men a final spray of bullets, then flew off in pursuit of the Bishop.

As he gave chase, he saw Virgil and Nimue in combat. Virgil moved deftly through the yolk, circling his foe along all axes of their liquid arena. He hacked at her spider legs with his sword. The legs were metal; they were her modified helicopter blades. The sword clanged against them ineffectually.

Nimue reared up, thrusting her genitals at Virgil. A tiny beak emerged from between her labia. It clucked, hostile.

Virgil froze.

The beak emerged further. Attached to the beak was a chicken. The chicken struggled out of Nimue. Slick with vaginal juice, it clucked.

It was Cleopatra. She had survived the attack on the trailer, escaping with Nimue. The witch had saved the chicken.

Now Jack learned why.

Cleopatra trembled and squawked as a monster was born from her anus. Nimue saw the monster and beamed; it seemed she had fathered more than one child that night in the chicken coop. Here, at last, was her firstborn.

For five seconds the witch child was just a giant maggot. Then it started to change. Jack watched, not comprehending. Virgil watched, not comprehending. Even the Bishop and the army of pig-men watched—not comprehending.

Tommy, comprehending, screamed louder.

The witch child flickered, phasing in and out. Parts of it existed in dimensions higher than the familiar three, and those parts could not be known or hypothesized.

Jack saw: a feathered dragon riddled with beaks, beaks that opened like windows onto a living boiler room where human eyeballs grew like soap bubbles; then the dragon turned and Jack saw that it was really a skyscraper on fire; then an origami swan on fire.

Nimue looked proud.

As anticipated, the witch child ate its mother. Cleopatra accepted this fate stoically. It seemed only natural.

Virgil regained his senses and raised his sword anew. He was not quick enough. The witch child decapitated him with a chainsaw-tipped tentacle. A frog tongue darted out from the feathered chest of the witch child; it caught the severed head, gathered it in as a morsel of food. The witch child finished off Virgil with its chainsaw, unzipping his molecules (the chainsaw was fractal—each tooth itself a miniature chainsaw, ad infinitum… good for subatomic work). Even without a head, Virgil somehow managed to scream as the saw erased him from existence.

Jack could not mourn. He sprayed the witch child with bullets. No effect.

Bishop Eichmann approached the witch child. He seemed to have forgotten all about Tommy. He gazed up at Nimue's offspring, eyes glassy and mouth slack. The witch child cycled through forms, becoming a lion, a golden city. Breathless, the Bishop inquired: "God?"

In answer, the golden city opened its gates.

The Bishop fell on his knees. "God!"

A frog tongue darted out through the gates. It seized the Bishop and drew him in. "Hallelujah!" the Bishop cried, a beatific smile on his pig face. "Hell yes!" The gates closed behind him, and the golden city convulsed back into a lion.

The lion burped.

THIRD SHIFT

Bishop Eichmann's legion of pig-men did not follow him into the golden city slash lion. They did not share his faith, it seemed. The witch child had no need for faith; it pounced upon the pig-men, sandpaper tongue lapping them up in pairs. They fled, it chased. The squeals were chilling.

Jack aimed his tommy gun into the fray. The gun clicked, out of ammo. He tossed it, spat out his cigar. He turned away from the massacre. The scene he turned to was no less full of wretched humanity.

Tommy was giving birth.

Jack rushed to his aid. He could think of nothing else to do.

Nimue was there already, ushering her second child into the world. She squatted behind Tommy, holding his buttocks open to see his sphincter. She said, "Ten centimeters—you're fully dilated! Push! Push!"

Tommy breathed, sweated. Jack got close and spoke frankly: "Your child is going to try to devour you, Tommy. I don't know if I can stop it."

Tommy whimpered.

Jack said, "There is one thing I need to know before you die. Please, tell me: what relation are you to the Bishop?"

Tommy spoke between contractions: "I'm, his, Tommy."

"Yes, but—"

"His TOM—Topologically Overlapping Morphism."

Jack said, "I have no education in theology or mathematics."

"Clone," Tommy said. "I'm, his, clone."

82

Tommy screamed. There was a wet ripping sound. Nimue screamed too, delighted. She emerged from behind Tommy, cradling a giant maggot.

Jack had no weapons. He took off his bowtie and rushed at the maggot, intending to strangle the maggot with the tie. Nimue warded him off with a spider leg. In her arms, the witch larva started to change.

It grew an enormous mouth. The mouth shot out elastically, swallowed Tommy whole, and snapped back into place.

Jack watched, feeling nothing. It was like watching a bird eat a bug.

The enormous mouth, having served its purpose, metamorphosed away.

The other witch child finished off the pig-men. It stalked toward Jack and Nimue. It was a feathered dragon again, a thing of eyeballs and fire. Jack still held his bowtie. He did not think he could strangle the dragon with it.

He put the bowtie back on. Might as well die looking good.

The dragon stopped. It wagged its tail like a dog. Nimue patted it on the head, and it nuzzled her. It nuzzled the witch child in her arms. It nuzzled Jack's buttocks and the fetal witch within.

Family.

The dragon groaned as its guts rumbled. Nimue looked at Jack, grinning, and said, "Indigestion." Like she thought it was cute.

But it was more than indigestion. The dragon hiccupped. A shadow crossed its face. Something was wrong inside.

The dragon grew a Hitler mustache.

Hitler mustaches erupted all over its body, sprouting like deadly tumors. The dragon shrieked in terror. It thrashed, spun, trying to escape what was happening.

No escape. The witch child disintegrated explosively, becoming water. It dissipated into the surrounding yolk. As if it had never been.

Nimue wept.

A voice said, "I too am bound to this sad fate."

Jack glanced down. The voice belonged to the witch child in Nimue's arms. It had shed its larval form completely, an adult now. It was nothing like its late half-sibling. It had the body of an elderly man but was still an infant in size. Rheumy eyes stared out from the thin, craggy flesh of its face. It said, "I near my terminus."

Nimue cradled the elderly infant, showering it with tears. "Not you too!"

"Weep not, father. I have loved my short life."

Jack said, "Why are you dying?"

"I ingested a toxic genome—the same toxic genome my late sibling ingested. The one called Eichmann." The elderly baby smirked. "In my larval stage, I had not the supreme intellect I have now. Blind instinct guided me, and I devoured my mother for his nutrients. And now those nutrients have doomed me!"

"Food poisoning?"

"*Field* poisoning. The morphic field of the Eichmann genome. It is undoing me, as it undid my sibling." The witch child coughed; its hands shook. "I suppose you *could* call it food poisoning. Fields, patterns—they are the food of actuality. To think—the most advanced beings in the universe, brought down by food poisoning!"

"We are what we eat."

"And I have eaten an Eichmann! A pattern of pure Nothing! Even a diet of holy water could not have reduced me to this end."

"I'm sorry," Jack said. "You seem really nice."

Nimue kissed the miniature old man on his forehead. "I love you!"

And then they waited. It didn't take long. The elderly infant coughed, trembled, and flatly intoned: "I am cancelled." Then it was gone, turned suddenly to water. The water dispersed into the surrounding yolk.

Nimue dried her tears. She and Jack were alone, suspended in the yolk of Nothing.

"I'm a failure as a father," she said.

"It's not your fault."

"A failure!"

"You're not a failure," Jack said, and he touched his belly.

She watched his hand rub up and down. "You don't want the baby," she reminded him. But there was a note of hope in her voice. "Don't pretend you do."

"I can accept having a child. I can accept disrupting the pattern called God. I never wanted to serve the status quo. I only wanted to not be eaten."

"New life always eats its source. Even if only figuratively. I can't stop it."

"I can't stop it either. And I can't stop the baby from being born. The holy water in my veins is getting weak; I can feel it losing ground to the new pattern emerging. So you see, you haven't failed. I have, but you haven't. And this child will have good food, not the poison Nothing of

Eichmann. I am not sure what I am, but I know I am not
Nothing. I am part of some pattern. I am going to give birth.
I am going to die. It's fate."

"I have you bewitched, Jack. You don't mean anything
you're saying."

"I know."

He thrust Excalibur at her, transmitting a thought: I
LOVE YOU.

She saw what he was trying to do. "The semen I took
from you is depleted. I can no longer scan your brainwaves."

"Oh. I said: I love you."

She grinned for a single frame. "You can name the child.
Call it anything you like."

"Let me think about it."

The night passed while Jack thought about it.

WEEKEND

Nimue rested her head on Jack, listening to the baby stir within him. "I think this one is going to be special," she said. "Greater even than its siblings." She had altered her metal appendages again, forming them not into helicopter blades or spider legs, but into the framework of a room. The versatile appendages even formed furniture for the room. It was all rather rickety, but it was theirs. Jack lay in a wiry bed, Nimue in a slanted chair beside him, a chair that grew out of her own back. She controlled the metal flesh of the furniture—rippling the bed to roll Jack onto his belly, reaching feelers from the wiry throng to slice away his lace panties and expose his butt. She listened again, analyzing the fetal sounds. Tweezing out the future. She smiled. "Jack, nothing this great has ever been born. Want to hear something funny? Our child is going to eat *both* of us. You alone will not be enough for it. In fact, you and I both will not be enough for it. It will consume this entire planet. All the planets. It must consume all that came before it as fuel for its greatness. This is so exciting, Jack!"

But Jack was beyond excitement; his mind was traveling out. He awoke to the colors of a new plane. He awoke on the cover of a magazine in the hands of everyone. He was not nauseous or afraid or jealous or annoyed. He was free, and a mother.

The maggot of blazing gold ate its mother. It ate its father and the room its father had built. Then it started on the surrounding yolk. It ran Tommy's emanation in reverse, consuming what he had produced: the yolk... the cysts of primordial tissue that condensed out of the yolk... the asteroids of emergent form that grew out of the primordial tissue... and, furthest out, the baroque assemblages of all that was latent in the emergent—in the primordial—in the yolk. All fell inward, sucked into the golden newborn as its first nourishment.

The newborn found a tether leading away through the void. A fragile umbilicus.

Then, as had not happened since the Old Eon, the Prisoner of Omega—Excalibur, it was called this time, in honor of its mother's penis—escaped into the world.

Andrew Wayne Adams was born and raised in rural Ohio. Growing up, he spent most of his time watching slasher films to feel less alone. His stories have appeared in a limited number of places throughout the years, and encountering one is like spotting a UFO. He is happy and successful.

Visit him online at: andrewwayneadams.blogspot.com

BIZARRO BOOKS

CATALOG   SPRING 2012

ERASERHEAD PRESS

Your major resource for the bizarro fiction genre:

WWW.BIZARROCENTRAL.COM

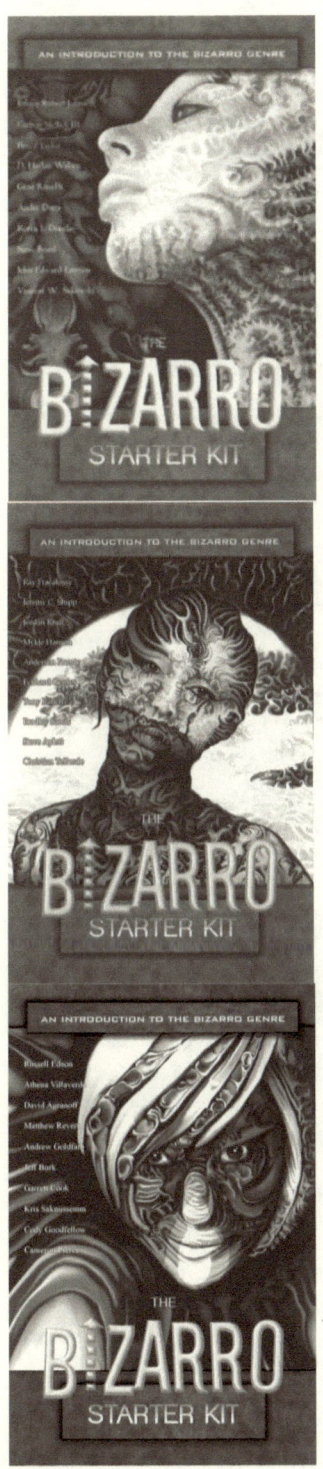

Introduce yourselves to the bizarro fiction genre and all of its authors with the Bizarro Starter Kit series. Each volume features short novels and short stories by ten of the leading bizarro authors, designed to give you a perfect sampling of the genre for only $10.

BB-0X1
"The Bizarro Starter Kit"
(Orange)
Featuring D. Harlan Wilson, Carlton Mellick III, Jeremy Robert Johnson, Kevin L Donihe, Gina Ranalli, Andre Duza, Vincent W. Sakowski, Steve Beard, John Edward Lawson, and Bruce Taylor.
236 pages $10

BB-0X2
"The Bizarro Starter Kit"
(Blue)
Featuring Ray Fracalossy, Jeremy C. Shipp, Jordan Krall, Mykle Hansen, Andersen Prunty, Eckhard Gerdes, Bradley Sands, Steve Aylett, Christian TeBordo, and Tony Rauch. **244 pages $10**

BB-0X2
"The Bizarro Starter Kit"
(Purple)
Featuring Russell Edson, Athena Villaverde, David Agranoff, Matthew Revert, Andrew Goldfarb, Jeff Burk, Garrett Cook, Kris Saknussemm, Cody Goodfellow, and Cameron Pierce **264 pages $10**

BB-001 **"The Kafka Effekt" D. Harlan Wilson** — A collection of forty-four irreal short stories loosely written in the vein of Franz Kafka, with more than a pinch of William S. Burroughs sprinkled on top. **211 pages $14**

BB-002 **"Satan Burger" Carlton Mellick III** — The cult novel that put Carlton Mellick III on the map ... Six punks get jobs at a fast food restaurant owned by the devil in a city violently overpopulated by surreal alien cultures. **236 pages $14**

BB-003 **"Some Things Are Better Left Unplugged" Vincent Sakwoski** — Join The Man and his Nemesis, the obese tabby, for a nightmare roller coaster ride into this postmodern fantasy. **152 pages $10**

BB-004 **"Shall We Gather At the Garden?" Kevin L Donihe** — Donihe's Debut novel. Midgets take over the world, The Church of Lionel Richie vs. The Church of the Byrds, plant porn and more! **244 pages $14**

BB-005 **"Razor Wire Pubic Hair" Carlton Mellick III** — A genderless humandildo is purchased by a razor dominatrix and brought into her nightmarish world of bizarre sex and mutilation. **176 pages $11**

BB-006 **"Stranger on the Loose" D. Harlan Wilson** — The fiction of Wilson's 2nd collection is planted in the soil of normalcy, but what grows out of that soil is a dark, witty, otherworldly jungle... **228 pages $14**

BB-007 **"The Baby Jesus Butt Plug" Carlton Mellick III** — Using clones of the Baby Jesus for anal sex will be the hip sex fetish of the future. **92 pages $10**

BB-008 **"Fishyfleshed" Carlton Mellick III** — The world of the past is an illogical flatland lacking in dimension and color, a sick-scape of crispy squid people wandering the desert for no apparent reason. **260 pages $14**

BB-009 **"Dead Bitch Army" Andre Duza** — Step into a world filled with racist teenagers, cannibals, 100 warped Uncle Sams, automobiles with razor-sharp teeth, living graffiti, and a pissed-off zombie bitch out for revenge. **344 pages $16**

BB-010 **"The Menstruating Mall" Carlton Mellick III** — "The Breakfast Club meets Chopping Mall as directed by David Lynch." - Brian Keene **212 pages $12**

BB-011 **"Angel Dust Apocalypse" Jeremy Robert Johnson** — Meth-heads, man-made monsters, and murderous Neo-Nazis. "Seriously amazing short stories..." - Chuck Palahniuk, author of Fight Club **184 pages $11**

BB-012 **"Ocean of Lard" Kevin L Donihe / Carlton Mellick III** — A parody of those old Choose Your Own Adventure kid's books about some very odd pirates sailing on a sea made of animal fat. **176 pages $12**

BB-015 **"Foop!" Chris Genoa** — Strange happenings are going on at Dactyl, Inc, the world's first and only time travel tourism company.
"A surreal pie in the face!" - Christopher Moore **300 pages $14**

BB-020 **"Punk Land" Carlton Mellick III** — In the punk version of Heaven, the anarchist utopia is threatened by corporate fascism and only Goblin, Mortician's sperm, and a blue-mohawked female assassin named Shark Girl can stop them. **284 pages $15**

BB-027 **"Siren Promised" Jeremy Robert Johnson & Alan M Clark** — Nominated for the Bram Stoker Award. A potent mix of bad drugs, bad dreams, brutal bad guys, and surreal/incredible art by Alan M. Clark. **190 pages $13**

BB-031**"Sea of the Patchwork Cats" Carlton Mellick III** — A quiet dreamlike tale set in the ashes of the human race. For Mellick enthusiasts who also adore The Twilight Zone. **112 pages $10**

BB-032 "Extinction Journals" Jeremy Robert Johnson — An uncanny voyage across a newly nuclear America where one man must confront the problems associated with loneliness, insane dieties, radiation, love, and an ever-evolving cockroach suit with a mind of its own. **104 pages $10**

BB-037 "The Haunted Vagina" Carlton Mellick III — It's difficult to love a woman whose vagina is a gateway to the world of the dead. **132 pages $10**

BB-043 "War Slut" Carlton Mellick III — Part "1984," part "Waiting for Godot," and part action horror video game adaptation of John Carpenter's "The Thing." **116 pages $10**

BB-047 "Sausagey Santa" Carlton Mellick III — A bizarro Christmas tale featuring Santa as a piratey mutant with a body made of sausages. 124 pages $10

BB-048 "Misadventures in a Thumbnail Universe" Vincent Sakowski — Dive deep into the surreal and satirical realms of neo-classical Blender Fiction, filled with television shoes and flesh-filled skies. **120 pages $10**

BB-053 "Ballad of a Slow Poisoner" Andrew Goldfarb — Millford Mutterwurst sat down on a Tuesday to take his afternoon tea, and made the unpleasant discovery that his elbows were becoming flatter. **128 pages $10**

BB-055 "Help! A Bear is Eating Me" Mykle Hansen — The bizarro, heartwarming, magical tale of poor planning, hubris and severe blood loss... **150 pages $11**

BB-056 "Piecemeal June" Jordan Krall — A man falls in love with a living sex doll, but with love comes danger when her creator comes after her with crab-squid assassins. **90 pages $9**

BB-058 **"The Overwhelming Urge" Andersen Prunty** — A collection of bizarro tales by Andersen Prunty. **150 pages $11**

BB-059 **"Adolf in Wonderland" Carlton Mellick III** — A dreamlike adventure that takes a young descendant of Adolf Hitler's design and sends him down the rabbit hole into a world of imperfection and disorder. **180 pages $11**

BB-061 **"Ultra Fuckers" Carlton Mellick III** — Absurdist suburban horror about a couple who enter an upper middle class gated community but can't find their way out. **108 pages $9**

BB-062 **"House of Houses" Kevin L. Donihe** — An odd man wants to marry his house. Unfortunately, all of the houses in the world collapse at the same time in the Great House Holocaust. Now he must travel to House Heaven to find his departed fiancee. **172 pages $11**

BB-064 **"Squid Pulp Blues" Jordan Krall** — In these three bizarro-noir novellas, the reader is thrown into a world of murderers, drugs made from squid parts, deformed gun-toting veterans, and a mischievous apocalyptic donkey. **204 pages $12**

BB-065 **"Jack and Mr. Grin" Andersen Prunty** — "When Mr. Grin calls you can hear a smile in his voice. Not a warm and friendly smile, but the kind that seizes your spine in fear. You don't need to pay your phone bill to hear it. That smile is in every line of Prunty's prose." - Tom Bradley. **208 pages $12**

BB-066 **"Cybernetrix" Carlton Mellick III** — What would you do if your normal everyday world was slowly mutating into the video game world from Tron? **212 pages $12**

BB-072 **"Zerostrata" Andersen Prunty** — Hansel Nothing lives in a tree house, suffers from memory loss, has a very eccentric family, and falls in love with a woman who runs naked through the woods every night. **144 pages $11**

BB-073 "The Egg Man" Carlton Mellick III — It is a world where humans reproduce like insects. Children are the property of corporations, and having an enormous ten-foot brain implanted into your skull is a grotesque sexual fetish. Mellick's industrial urban dystopia is one of his darkest and grittiest to date. **184 pages $11**

BB-074 "Shark Hunting in Paradise Garden" Cameron Pierce — A group of strange humanoid religious fanatics travel back in time to the Garden of Eden to discover it is invested with hundreds of giant flying maneating sharks. **150 pages $10**

BB-075 "Apeshit" Carlton Mellick III - Friday the 13th meets Visitor Q. Six hipster teens go to a cabin in the woods inhabited by a deformed killer. An incredibly fucked-up parody of B-horror movies with a bizarro slant. **192 pages $12**

BB-076 "Fuckers of Everything on the Crazy Shitting Planet of the Vomit At smosphere" Mykle Hansen - Three bizarro satires. Monster Cocks, Journey to the Center of Agnes Cuddlebottom, and Crazy Shitting Planet. **228 pages $12**

BB-077 "The Kissing Bug" Daniel Scott Buck — In the tradition of Roald Dahl, Tim Burton, and Edward Gorey, comes this bizarro anti-war children's story about a bohemian conenose kissing bug who falls in love with a human woman. **116 pages $10**

BB-078 "MachoPoni" Lotus Rose — It's My Little Pony... *Bizarro* style! A long time ago Poniworld was split in two. On one side of the Jagged Line is the Pastel Kingdom, a magical land of music, parties, and positivity. On the other side of the Jagged Line is Dark Kingdom inhabited by an army of undead ponies. **148 pages $11**

BB-079 "The Faggiest Vampire" Carlton Mellick III — A Roald Dahl-esque children's story about two faggy vampires who partake in a mustache competition to find out which one is truly the faggiest. **104 pages $10**

BB-080 "Sky Tongues" Gina Ranalli — The autobiography of Sky Tongues, the biracial hermaphrodite actress with tongues for fingers. Follow her strange life story as she rises from freak to fame. **204 pages $12**

BB-081 **"Washer Mouth" Kevin L. Donihe** - A washing machine becomes human and pursues his dream of meeting his favorite soap opera star. **244 pages $11**

BB-082 **"Shatnerquake" Jeff Burk** - All of the characters ever played by William Shatner are suddenly sucked into our world. Their mission: hunt down and destroy the real William Shatner. **100 pages $10**

BB-083 **"The Cannibals of Candyland" Carlton Mellick III** - There exists a race of cannibals that are made of candy. They live in an underground world made out of candy. One man has dedicated his life to killing them all. **170 pages $11**

BB-084 **"Slub Glub in the Weird World of the Weeping Willows"** **Andrew Goldfarb** - The charming tale of a blue glob named Slub Glub who helps the weeping willows whose tears are flooding the earth. There are also hyenas, ghosts, and a voodoo priest **100 pages $10**

BB-085 **"Super Fetus" Adam Pepper** - Try to abort this fetus and he'll kick your ass! **104 pages $10**

BB-086 **"Fistful of Feet" Jordan Krall** - A bizarro tribute to spaghetti westerns, featuring Cthulhu-worshipping Indians, a woman with four feet, a crazed gunman who is obsessed with sucking on candy, Syphilis-ridden mutants, sexually transmitted tattoos, and a house devoted to the freakiest fetishes. **228 pages $12**

BB-087 **"Ass Goblins of Auschwitz" Cameron Pierce** - It's Monty Python meets Nazi exploitation in a surreal nightmare as can only be imagined by Bizarro author Cameron Pierce. **104 pages $10**

BB-088 **"Silent Weapons for Quiet Wars" Cody Goodfellow** - "This is high-end psychological surrealist horror meets bottom-feeding low-life crime in a techno-thrilling science fiction world full of Lovecraft and magic..." -John Skipp **212 pages $12**

BB-089 "Warrior Wolf Women of the Wasteland" Carlton Mellick III
— Road Warrior Werewolves versus McDonaldland Mutants...post-apocalyptic fiction has never been quite like this. **316 pages $13**

BB-091 "Super Giant Monster Time" Jeff Burk — A tribute to choose your own adventures and Godzilla movies. Will you escape the giant monsters that are rampaging the fuck out of your city and shit? Or will you join the mob of alien-controlled punk rockers causing chaos in the streets? What happens next depends on you. **188 pages $12**

BB-092 "Perfect Union" Cody Goodfellow — "Cronenberg's THE FLY on a grand scale: human/insect gene-spliced body horror, where the human hive politics are as shocking as the gore." -John Skipp. **272 pages $13**

BB-093 "Sunset with a Beard" Carlton Mellick III — 14 stories of surreal science fiction. **200 pages $12**

BB-094 "My Fake War" Andersen Prunty — The absurd tale of an unlikely soldier forced to fight a war that, quite possibly, does not exist. It's Rambo meets Waiting for Godot in this subversive satire of American values and the scope of the human imagination. **128 pages $11**

BB-095 "Lost in Cat Brain Land" Cameron Pierce — Sad stories from a surreal world. A fascist mustache, the ghost of Franz Kafka, a desert inside a dead cat. Primordial entities mourn the death of their child. The desperate serve tea to mysterious creatures. A hopeless romantic falls in love with a pterodactyl. And much more. **152 pages $11**

BB-096 "The Kobold Wizard's Dildo of Enlightenment +2" Carlton Mellick III — A Dungeons and Dragons parody about a group of people who learn they are only made up characters in an AD&D campaign and must find a way to resist their nerdy teenaged players and retarded dungeon master in order to survive. **232 pages $12**

BB-098 "A Hundred Horrible Sorrows of Ogner Stump" Andrew Goldfarb — Goldfarb's acclaimed comic series. A magical and weird journey into the horrors of everyday life. **164 pages $11**

BB-099 **"Pickled Apocalypse of Pancake Island" Cameron Pierce**—A demented fairy tale about a pickle, a pancake, and the apocalypse. **102 pages $8**

BB-100 **"Slag Attack" Andersen Prunty**— Slag Attack features four visceral, noir stories about the living, crawling apocalypse.A slag is what survivors are calling the slug-like maggots raining from the sky, burrowing inside people, and hollowing out their flesh and their sanity. **148 pages $11**

BB-101 **"Slaughterhouse High" Robert Devereaux**—A place where schools are built with secret passageways, rebellious teens get zippers installed in their mouths and genitals, and once a year, on that special night, one couple is slaughtered and the bits of their bodies are kept as souvenirs. **304 pages $13**

BB-102 **"The Emerald Burrito of Oz" John Skipp & Marc Levinthal** —OZ IS REAL! Magic is real! The gate is really in Kansas! And America is finally allowing Earth tourists to visit this weird-ass, mysterious land. But when Gene of Los Angeles heads off for summer vacation in the Emerald City, little does he know that a war is brewing...a war that could destroy both worlds. **280 pages $13**

BB-103 **"The Vegan Revolution... with Zombies" David Agranoff** — When there's no more meat in hell, the vegans will walk the earth. **160 pages $11**

BB-104 **"The Flappy Parts" Kevin L Donihe**—Poems about bunnies, LSD, and police abuse. You know, things that matter. 132 **pages $11**

BB-105 **"Sorry I Ruined Your Orgy" Bradley Sands**—Bizarro humorist Bradley Sands returns with one of the strangest, most hilarious collections of the year. **130 pages $11**

BB-106 **"Mr. Magic Realism" Bruce Taylor**—Like Golden Age science fiction comics written by Freud, *Mr. Magic Realism* is a strange, insightful adventure that spans the furthest reaches of the galaxy, exploring the hidden caverns in the hearts and minds of men, women, aliens, and biomechanical cats. **152 pages $11**

BB-107 "Zombies and Shit" Carlton Mellick III—"Battle Royale" meets "Return of the Living Dead." Mellick's bizarro tribute to the zombie genre. **308 pages $13**

BB-108 "The Cannibal's Guide to Ethical Living" Mykle Hansen— Over a five star French meal of fine wine, organic vegetables and human flesh, a lunatic delivers a witty, chilling, disturbingly sane argument in favor of eating the rich.. **184 pages $11**

BB-109 "Starfish Girl" Athena Villaverde—In a post-apocalyptic underwater dome society, a girl with a starfish growing from her head and an assassin with sea anenome hair are on the run from a gang of mutant fish men. **160 pages $11**

BB-110 "Lick Your Neighbor" Chris Genoa—Mutant ninjas, a talking whale, kung fu masters, maniacal pilgrims, and an alcoholic clown populate Chris Genoa's surreal, darkly comical and unnerving reimagining of the first Thanksgiving. **303 pages $13**

BB-111 "Night of the Assholes" Kevin L. Donihe—A plague of assholes is infecting the countryside. Normal everyday people are transforming into jerks, snobs, dicks, and douchebags. And they all have only one purpose: to make your life a living hell.. **192 pages $11**

BB-112 "Jimmy Plush, Teddy Bear Detective" Garrett Cook—Hardboiled cases of a private detective trapped within a teddy bear body. **180 pages $11**

BB-113 "The Deadheart Shelters" Forrest Armstrong—The hip hop lovechild of William Burroughs and Dali... **144 pages $11**

BB-114 "Eyeballs Growing All Over Me... Again" Tony Raugh— Absurd, surreal, playful, dream-like, whimsical, and a lot of fun to read. **144 pages $11**

BB-115 **"Whargoul" Dave Brockie** — From the killing grounds of Stalingrad to the death camps of the holocaust. From torture chambers in Iraq to race riots in the United States, the Whargoul was there, killing and raping. **244 pages $12**

BB-116 "By the Time We Leave Here, We'll Be Friends" J. David Osborne — A David Lynchian nightmare set in a Russian gulag, where its prisoners, guards, traitors, soldiers, lovers, and demons fight for survival and their own rapidly deteriorating humanity. **168 pages $11**

BB-117 "Christmas on Crack" edited by Carlton Mellick III — Perverted Christmas Tales for the whole family! . . . as long as every member of your family is over the age of 18. **168 pages $11**

BB-118 "Crab Town" Carlton Mellick III — Radiation fetishists, balloon people, mutant crabs, sail-bike road warriors, and a love affair between a woman and an H-Bomb. This is one mean asshole of a city. Welcome to Crab Town. **100 pages $8**

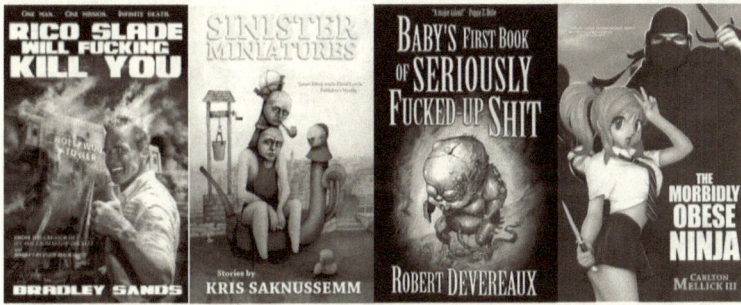

BB-119 "Rico Slade Will Fucking Kill You" Bradley Sands — Rico Slade is an action hero. Rico Slade can rip out a throat with his bare hands. Rico Slade's favorite food is the honey-roasted peanut. Rico Slade will fucking kill everyone. A novel. **122 pages $8**

BB-120 "Sinister Miniatures" Kris Saknussemm — The definitive collection of short fiction by Kris Saknussemm, confirming that he is one of the best, most daring writers of the weird to emerge in the twenty-first century. **180 pages $11**

BB-121 "Baby's First Book of Seriously Fucked up Shit" Robert Devereaux — Ten stories of the strange, the gross, and the just plain fucked up from one of the most original voices in horror. **176 pages $11**

BB-122 "The Morbidly Obese Ninja" Carlton Mellick III — These days, if you want to run a successful company . . . you're going to need a lot of ninjas. **92 pages $8**

BB-123 **"Abortion Arcade" Cameron Pierce** — An intoxicating blend of body horror and midnight movie madness, reminiscent of early David Lynch and the splatterpunks at their most sublime. **172 pages $11**

BB-124 **"Black Hole Blues" Patrick Wensink** — A hilarious double helix of country music and physics. **196 pages $11**

BB-125 **"Barbarian Beast Bitches of the Badlands" Carlton Mellick III** — Three prequels and sequels to *Warrior Wolf Women of the Wasteland*. **284 pages $13**

BB-126 **"The Traveling Dildo Salesman" Kevin L. Donihe** — A nightmare comedy about destiny, faith, and sex toys. Also featuring Donihe's most lurid and infamous short stories: *Milky Agitation, Two-Way Santa, The Helen Mower, Living Room Zombies*, and *Revenge of the Living Masturbation Rag*. **108 pages $8**

BB-127 **"Metamorphosis Blues" Bruce Taylor** — Enter a land of love beasts, intergalactic cowboys, and rock 'n roll. A land where Sears Catalogs are doorways to insanity and men keep mysterious black boxes. Welcome to the monstrous mind of Mr. Magic Realism. **136 pages $11**

BB-128 **"The Driver's Guide to Hitting Pedestrians" Andersen Prunty** — A pocket guide to the twenty-three most painful things in life, written by the most well-adjusted man in the universe. **108 pages $8**

BB-129 **"Island of the Super People" Kevin Shamel** — Four students and their anthropology professor journey to a remote island to study its indigenous population. But this is no ordinary native culture. They're super heroes and villains with flesh costumes and outlandish abilities like self-detonation, musical eyelashes, and microwave hands. **194 pages $11**

BB-130 **"Fantastic Orgy" Carlton Mellick III** — Shark Sex, mutant cats, and strange sexually transmitted diseases. Featuring the stories: *Candy-coated, Ear Cat, Fantastic Orgy, City Hobgoblins*, and *Porno in August*. **136 pages $9**

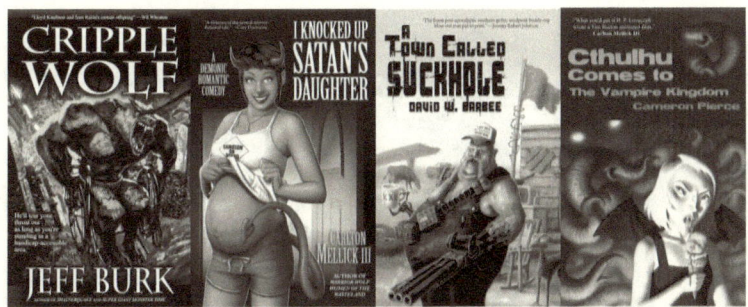

BB-131 **"Cripple Wolf" Jeff Burk** — Part man. Part wolf. 100% crippled. Also including *Punk Rock Nursing Home, Adrift with Space Badgers, Cook for Your Life, Just Another Day in the Park, Frosty and the Full Monty*, and *House of Cats*. **152 pages $10**

BB-132 **"I Knocked Up Satan's Daughter" Carlton Mellick III** — An adorable, violent, fantastical love story. A romantic comedy for the bizarro fiction reader. **152 pages $10**

BB-133 **"A Town Called Suckhole" David W. Barbee** — Far into the future, in the nuclear bowels of post-apocalyptic Dixie, there is a town. A town of derelict mobile homes, ancient junk, and mutant wildlife. A town of slack jawed rednecks who bask in the splendors of moonshine and mud boggin'. A town dedicated to the bloody and demented legacy of the Old South. A town called Suckhole. **144 pages $10**

BB-134 **"Cthulhu Comes to the Vampire Kingdom" Cameron Pierce** — What you'd get if H. P. Lovecraft wrote a Tim Burton animated film. **148 pages $11**

BB-135 **"I am Genghis Cum" Violet LeVoit** — From the savage Arctic tundra to post-partum mutations to your missing daughter's unmarked grave, join visionary madwoman Violet LeVoit in this non-stop eight-story onslaught of full-tilt Bizarro punk lit thrills. **124 pages $9**

BB-136 **"Haunt" Laura Lee Bahr** — A tripping-balls Los Angeles noir, where a mysterious dame drags you through a time-warping Bizarro hall of mirrors. **316 pages $13**

BB-137 **"Amazing Stories of the Flying Spaghetti Monster" edited by Cameron Pierce** — Like an all-spaghetti evening of Adult Swim, the Flying Spaghetti Monster will show you the many realms of His Noodly Appendage. Learn of those who worship him and the lives he touches in distant, mysterious ways. **228 pages $12**

BB-138 **"Wave of Mutilation" Douglas Lain** — A dream-pop exploration of modern architecture and the American identity, *Wave of Mutilation* is a Zen finger trap for the 21st century. **100 pages $8**

BB-139 **"Hooray for Death!" Mykle Hansen** — Famous Author Mykle Hansen draws unconventional humor from deaths tiny and large, and invites you to laugh while you can. **128 pages $10**

BB-140 **"Hypno-hog's Moonshine Monster Jamboree" Andrew Goldfarb** — Hicks, Hogs, Horror! Goldfarb is back with another strange illustrated tale of backwoods weirdness. **120 pages $9**

BB-141 **"Broken Piano For President" Patrick Wensink** — A comic masterpiece about the fast food industry, booze, and the necessity to choose happiness over work and security. **372 pages $15**

BB-142 **"Please Do Not Shoot Me in the Face" Bradley Sands** — A novel in three parts, *Please Do Not Shoot Me in the Face: A Novel*, is the story of one boy detective, the worst ninja in the world, and the great American fast food wars. It is a novel of loss, destruction, and--incredibly--genuine hope. **224 pages $12**

BB-143 **"Santa Steps Out" Robert Devereaux** — Sex, Death, and Santa Claus ... The ultimate erotic Christmas story is back. **294 pages $13**

BB-144 **"Santa Conquers the Homophobes" Robert Devereaux** — "I wish I could hope to ever attain one-thousandth the perversity of Robert Devereaux's toenail clippings." - Poppy Z. Brite **316 pages $13**

BB-145 **"We Live Inside You" Jeremy Robert Johnson** — "Jeremy Robert Johnson is dancing to a way different drummer. He loves language, he loves the edge, and he loves us people. These stories have range and style and wit. This is entertainment... and literature."- Jack Ketchum **188 pages $11**

BB-146 **"Clockwork Girl" Athena Villaverde** — Urban fairy tales for the weird girl in all of us. Like a combination of Francesca Lia Block, Charles de Lint, Kathe Koja, Tim Burton, and Hayao Miyazaki, her stories are cute, kinky, edgy, magical, provocative, and strange, full of poetic imagery and vicious sexuality. **160 pages $10**

BB-147 "Armadillo Fists" Carlton Mellick III — A weird-as-hell gangster story set in a world where people drive giant mechanical dinosaurs instead of cars. **168 pages $11**

BB-148 "Gargoyle Girls of Spider Island" Cameron Pierce — Four college seniors venture out into open waters for the tropical party weekend of a life-time. Instead of a teenage sex fantasy, they find themselves in a nightmare of pirates, sharks, and sex-crazed monsters. **100 pages $8**

BB-149 "The Handsome Squirm" by Carlton Mellick III — Like Franz Kafka's *The Trial* meets an erotic body horror version of *The Blob*. **158 pages $11**

BB-150 "Tentacle Death Trip" Jordan Krall — It's *Death Race 2000* meets H. P. Lovecraft in bizarro author Jordan Krall's best and most suspenseful work to date. **224 pages $12**

BB-151 "The Obese" Nick Antosca — Like Alfred Hitchcock's *The Birds*... but with obese people. **108 pages $10**

BB-152 "All-Monster Action!" Cody Goodfellow — The world gave him a blank check and a demand: Create giant monsters to fight our wars. But Dr. Otaku was not satisfied with mere chaos and mass destruction.... **216 pages $12**

BB-153 "Ugly Heaven" Carlton Mellick III — Heaven is no longer a para-dise. It was once a blissful utopia full of wonders far beyond human comprehension. But the afterlife is now in ruins. It has become an ugly, lonely wasteland populated by strange monstrous beasts, masturbating angels, and sad man-like beings wallowing in the remains of the once-great Kingdom of God. **106 pages $8**

BB-154 "Space Walrus" Kevin L. Donihe — Walter is supposed to go where no walrus has ever gone before, but all this astronaut walrus really wants is to take it easy on the intense training, escape the chimpanzee bullies, and win the love of his human trainer Dr. Stephanie. **160 pages $11**

* 9 7 8 1 6 2 1 0 5 0 6 9 8 *